BIBLIOGRAPHIES IN AMERICAN MUSIC

Editor James R. Heintze
The American University

Ernst C. Krohn, at the Kunkel home library, 1951

MUSIC PUBLISHING IN ST. LOUIS

Ernst C. Krohn

(1888-1975)

completed and edited by

J. Bunker Clark

BIBLIOGRAPHIES IN AMERICAN MUSIC   NUMBER ELEVEN
PUBLISHED FOR THE COLLEGE MUSIC SOCIETY
HARMONIE PARK PRESS   1988

Printed and bound in the United States of America
Published by
Harmonie Park Press (*formerly* Information Coordinators)
23630 Pinewood
Warren, Michigan 48091

Editor, J. Bunker Clark
Art Director, Nicholas Jakubiak
Book design and Typography, J. Bunker Clark

Library of Congress Cataloging in Publication Data

    Krohn, Ernst C. (Ernst Christopher), 1888-1975.
       Music publishing in St. Louis.

       (Bibliographies in American music ; no. 11)
       "Published for the College Music Society."
       Includes bibliographical references and indexes.
       1. Music—Publishing—Missouri—St. Louis—History.
    1. Clark, J. Bunker. II. Title. III. Title:
    Music publishing in Saint Louis. IV. Series.
    ML112.K738 1988   070.5'794'0977866   88-21240
    ISBN 0-89990-043-7

CONTENTS

LIST OF ILLUSTRATIONS

Ernst C. Krohn, in his library, 1969

FOREWORD

by Lincoln Bunce Spiess

Ernst Krohn was one of the most remarkable individuals a person could have known in a lifetime. He was almost entirely self-taught--at least insofar as musicology is concerned, but to a large extent in other subjects as well--yet our many pleasant evenings of conversation over the years always would cover a wide variety of subjects. His immense library was primarily on music, though it contained also much on such varied subjects as drama, Indians of New Mexico, the Spanish Southwest, European and American painting, printing in this country, etc. The library reflected his view that musicology should never be limited to the confines of a musical page, but must learn from related areas. For example, his favorite subjects are illustrative: How could we understand American Indian music without understanding Indian culture in its many ramifications? How can one fully appreciate the development of American music divorced from American culture and history? In that way passed those many evenings of discussion and good conversation, pursuing the ramifications of such questions, and many, many more of like nature.

I first came to know Ernst in 1951 when I moved to St. Louis. He then lived on Juniata Street in the south part of the city, in a house built near the turn of the century. It was lined with books and music in every room, from attic to cellar, the result of a lifetime of collecting. His primary interest throughout the years that I knew him was in music of the Midwest, and particularly St. Louis and Missouri. He had written a small history of music in Missouri which was expanded some years before his death into *Missouri Music*. He would repeatedly talk about the various midwest music publishers from the early *Missouri Harmony* of the 1820s through the sheet music publishers and editions of the last century and into our time. His knowledge of that field was really unplumbable, and in conversation one could only see the "tip of the iceberg," as it were. Whether he had in his mind a book on the subject in the beginning, or at what point the knowledge began to be research for such a book, one could not say for sure. But the notebooks full of notes finally seemed to become notebooks full of an organized book. A preliminary small publication on midwestern music publishing finally reached print, and about that time he began sending the notebooks of the larger St. Louis publishing manuscript to prospective editors. I can recall the irritation he would express over rejection of the manuscript, usually the rejection being stated by the potential publisher as because of "its narrow regional nature." Now, of course, we are beginning to realize the very importance of such regional publications--as he always did himself (he had a complete collection of such regional books on American music). In a sense, his vision of the importance of such studies is now being vindicated.

In the 1960s Ernst, his sister, and his niece (the Marners), moved to Webster Groves, a pleasant suburb of St. Louis, to a charming house set amid trees and greenery, with garden and many birds, an ideal bucolic atmosphere for thought and writing, not to mention for pleasant conversation. (The music publishing manuscripts were completed there.) The new home wasn't quite adequate to house his library properly, and for the first time Ernst succumbed to persuasion to sell his collection to Gaylord Music Library, Washington University, St. Louis. The sale and terms were finally agreed by the university in late December 1966, and the writer received a phone call from the university while at the American Musicological Society convention in New Orleans, just before New Year's. Naturally I immediately called Ernst to let him know the good news--a New Year's present to cap the year! For a time, though, this development proved a mixed blessing, for his beloved library was leaving his home. But we assuaged that feeling of loss by making him honorary curator of the collection, and then engaged him to organize the combined sheet music collection, that of his own with that of Gaylord. It was during those years of organizing the combined collections that the final stages of his two music publishing studies probably crystallized.

In 1974 the family moved to Santa Fe, New Mexico, to an attractive home overlooking the foothills of his beloved Sangre de Cristo Mountains. For a time his health survived the move reasonably well, but an unexpected fall brought on complications and he never lived to see the St. Louis music publishing book into print. The manuscript, consequently, came to Gaylord and seemed destined to remain in the archives, to be seen only by an occasional researcher. The present plan to publish the work would have made him most happy, and vindicates his lifelong devotion to the importance of St. Louis in the development of American music.

St. Louis
November 1979

AN EMERGENT MUSICOLOGIST IN THE MIDDLE WEST

by Ernst C. Krohn

The contemporary wealth of foundation grants, the existence of extensive musicological libraries, the bewildering activities of swarms of musicologists may blind the current crop of graduate students in musicology to the fact that things were not always so lush.

Going to St. Louis from New York in 1899, I had to give up my high school career before the first year was up because of financial stringency in my family. I gave up my scholastic career reluctantly and ever after regarded the academic world as a lost paradise which I would somehow or other regain. Once in the commercial world I soon discovered that the basic philosophy of the business world was foreign to my conception of life. I soon resolved to study systematically to prepare myself for a teaching career, specifically in history. I read through all six of the Rawlinson volumes on the ancient oriental monarchies and was about to tackle Grote's Greek history when a well-meaning friend pointed out that I could never hope to teach in an academic institution without a graduate degree. Why didn't I get into music teaching which could be managed without any entrance examinations. I had studied piano with my father, who was a fine musician but a poor financier. I began practicing like mad when I decided on this alternative course of action. By this time I was working in the music store of Adam Shattinger. He laid me off for a few weeks in the summer of 1909 and I took advantage of my brief vacation, and through house-to-house solicitation acquired enough students to triple my income within those few precious weeks. I soon discovered that my father's training had its limitations and sought another teacher. By this time I become an addict to what Breithaupt terms *die natürliche Klaviertechnik*, and consequently I was particular about the type of piano teaching I wanted to indulge in. I found a satisfactory teacher in Ottmar Moll who had just returned from five years of study with Varette Stepanoff in Berlin. After five years of study with Moll, I gave my first piano recital in 1913 and was made his first assistant. We taught together happily until his death in 1934 when I inherited his studio furnishings and a large part of his class.

Meanwhile I had not been idle in a musicological sense. My work at the Shattinger store was that of order clerk. I had to familiarize myself with the catalogs of all the great editions in order to be able to procure immediately those items that our customers demanded. I soon acquired an impressive collection of catalogs, not only of music publishers but of book dealers as well. I began buying books, for the local libraries did not possess the books I thought that I should have. I became impressed with the need of putting down my bibliographical notions and soon finished an essay on *The Bibliography of Music* which was accepted by Oscar Sonneck for publication in *The Musical Quarterly*. I still cherish the galley proofs of my essay with Sonneck's autograph additions and comments. Sonneck became my god, and I bought and read everything he wrote that was then available. In 1924 the MTNA met in St. Louis and I read a paper on the development of the city's symphony orchestra. I met Waldo Selden Pratt, Charles Boyd, and Lota Spell, and was accepted by them as a fellow musicologist.

The work on my article on bibliography had made me aware of the requirements of a musicological library, and I planned my book purchases with great care. I had asked the acquisitions clerk at the Public Library to buy Adler's *Handbuch*. She told me that hers was a public library and not a specialist's collection and that if I wanted Adler to buy it myself. I did so and have been buying ever since. My program of book buying proved so effective that I recently sold my library to Washington University for a large enough sum to enable me to live the rest of my days in comfort and still be able to buy books that I require in my studies. Buying books has become a way of life. One day I received a letter from a Chicago dealer offering me a copy of Lyon's *Urania*. I bought it. Immediately he offered the *Scottish Musical Museum* published in Philadelphia in 1792. I bought it too and soon discovered that my copy was unique. In fact it was not until a few years ago that the Winterthur Museum picked up another copy. The catalog of the Wolffheim sale listed a complete run of *Monatshefte für Musikgeschichte*. I placed my bid with Liepmannssohn and acquired it. My set is probably the finest in existence. It was started by James Matthew, the English collector, and continued by Wolffheim, and includes everything. The books are bound in a lovely red morocco and are in pristine condition. The German binder was able to match the back imprint perfectly so that the binding is truly uniform. Liepmannssohn is one of the truly great men in musicology and his catalogs are of the utmost bibliographical importance. Modern parallels are those of Hans Schneider.

St. Louis is a comparatively old city and has a long bookish history; consequently the bookshops in the early 1900s were well supplied with music literature. Since this was a drug on the market at the time, I was able to pick up many choice items right here in my home town. I remember walking into Miner's book shop and his asking me the value of a copy of the 1776 edition of Morley's Practical Music. I told him it was worth about sixty dollars which I could not afford to pay. He said that it was the last book left of a large historical library he had just sold, and would two bucks be too much! At another time a downtown dealer acquired a copy of the elephant folio Festschrift issued by Milan for the meeting in 1892. He wanted sixty dollars for it. I offered him five. He put it in his show window for two weeks and finally begged me to take it off his hands at my price. It took me ten years to pick up a complete run of the publications of the International Music Society. Liepmannssohn was very helpful in this project.

I soon found it necessary to card-index the contents of the musicological journals that were piling up in my library. The depression of 1929-30 came in handy. Many of my pupils lost their jobs. I kept on teaching them. They offered to help me in payment for their lessons. Since most of them were typists I put them to work indexing. I soon had a girl working every day of the week. Some of them typed all day in payment for one piano lesson. One Italian girl proved particularly expert in copying the German titles in *Die Musik*. In the course of time I accumulated a periodical index running to one hundred thousand cards. One day Jerrold Orne, librarian at Washington University, was looking over my file. He offered to print as much of an index as he could with the thousand dollars left in his budget. In this way my Index to the History of Music came to light. I had material for five more volumes--but no publisher was available, nor has there been one since.

In 1922, Ernest R. Kroeger was asked to write an article on a Century of Missouri Music. It was the centennial of Missouri's admission to statehood. He was too busy at the time so he asked me to do the job. By the simple expedient of having the printer run off two hundred offprints of each of the three articles, and then printing the conclusion and index at my own expense, I soon had a book in a limited, numbered edition.

My interest in Alexander Reinagle runs back to my Sonneck days. Fascinated by his listing of the manuscript sonatas in the Library of Congress, I soon had photostats made of everything and got busy on the research that was to end in my essay on Reinagle in *The Musical Quarterly*. The limitations on musicological research in St. Louis came through in the article. There was then no comprehensive collection of Haydn symphonies in St. Louis. Consequently I did not know that the lovely Andante copied by Reinagle and inserted in the autograph of one of his sonatas was really from a Haydn symphony. M. Herter Norton tactfully corrected my error in the next issue, but it was nevertheless an embarrassing mistake to make.

When the depression was at its height I sat in my deserted studio meditating on the sad state of affairs. The notion came to me that I might fill in my time by lecturing on music. It never occurred to me that if I could not get one pupil at a time how could I get forty. I planned a ten-lecture course and got out announcements. To my surprise I soon had a class of forty, mostly my own colleagues in the teaching field. The course was a great success. The next year I gave a fifteen-lecture course. By basing my course on Adler's subdivision I found it capable of indefinite expansion. I soon was giving a thirty-lecture course. This was expanded to sixty and finally to one hundred and five. Meanwhile Dean Starbird of Washington University, whose mother was a member of one of my classes, called my course to the attention of Dean Debatin of University College. He called me in to become acquainted with my work and promptly engaged me to teach in University College. I taught there for fifteen years, at the end of which time I was invited by St. Louis University to head their music department. When I told the Jesuit who was engaging me that I had no degrees he just laughed. He told me that the last five music teachers all had degrees but they were no good. He assured me that if I could teach music the way they wanted it taught, I was the man they were looking for. They were so satisfied with the way I taught that they did not retire me until I was seventy-five.

Installed at St. Louis University, I soon heard about their microfilm project in the Vatican libraries. When I enquired what they were doing in music, the Jesuit in charge assured me that he had been to Rome and back again without anyone being able to tell him what to do about music. He assured me that if I could tell him what to microfilm he would do so. This was a definite challenge. I spent the next few years studying Vatican printed and manuscript catalogs for musical items. I also examined all the musicological literature available, looking for references to Vatican music manuscripts. I finally came up with a list of fifteen hundred items, most of which were microfilmed and are now available. I started to make a thematic catalog but soon found that that was an impossible task. I then contented myself with making an inventory of the contents of the rolls of microfilm available. The film, originally in one-hundred-foot rolls, had been cut up and spliced together to.form smaller rolls. One act of an opera would be in one roll, the second in still another, and the third in a different one. In the course of my inventory, which was never completed, I made many discoveries. I discovered some missing Stradella chamber cantatas which were only imperfectly listed by Hess. I discovered the Legrenzi oratorio *Sedicia* which is listed in MGG as *verschollen*. I copied this completely, intending to write it up but have never finished my research on the subject. Whatever I am doing has always been interrupted by something else that I was obliged to do.

Da Capo Press decided to reprint my *Century of Missouri Music* but asked me to bring it up to date. This involved a restudy of the local scene on a more intensive scale than I had done heretofore. Since I am practically the last of the Mohicans it is essential that I record what has happened here during my lifetime. St. Louis has been the cradle of culture in the Middle West since its foundation in 1764. Its musical history has been completely overlooked by most eastern historians. When John Tasker Howard wrote *Our American Music*, he wrote to me for detailed information. I gave him what he requested but he used my data in a completely incorrect manner. When I corrected his misstatements, he retaliated by mentioning St. Louis in a more inadequate manner than before. The importance of American studies to American musicology is still only dimly perceived by eastern historians. The time will come when European themes become threadworn. It will then be time for our prospective doctoral candidates to devote more of their energy to the American scene.

Ernst C. Krohn, in his library, 1971

EDITOR'S PREFACE

For St. Louis, I have just finished a study of "Nathaniel Phillips: The First Music Publisher in St. Louis," in addition to doing a vast amount of preparatory research for my projected book *Music Publishing in St. Louis.*

--Ernst C. Krohn, *Music Publishing in the Middle Western States before the Civil War* (1972), Prelude, 11.

I first learned of the 21 March 1975 death of Ernst C. Krohn from Lincoln Spiess, at the meeting of the Midwest Chapter of the American Musicological Society in Indianapolis that following April 24th. Professor Spiess also mentioned to me an unpublished manuscript by Mr. Krohn, about which my interest grew greater after becoming co-editor of *Bibliographies in American Music* that fall. I finally wrote to Betty Krause, librarian at the Gaylord Music Library, Washington University, in the summer of 1978, and the following October she graciously allowed me to take a duplicate copy to examine in detail. I soon discovered that the biggest problem was the lack of footnotes.

Mr. Krohn, probably sometime in 1974, had sent the manuscript to one university press, but it was rejected in January 1975, partly because it was not annotated. In retrospect, I suspect that he was trying to supply these in the months before he died. By a stroke of good fortune, Gloria Lamm had been involved with the moving of Mr. Krohn's library from the home of his niece Miss Doris Marner in Santa Fe, New Mexico, where he had retired, to the Gaylord Music Library where she was a staff member. She subsequently became a student assistant in the music library of the University of Kansas, where I got to know her. She aided considerably in answering questions about the state of the manuscript, and in procuring additional pages of the previous versions of *Music Publishing in St. Louis.*

In the fall of 1979, while on sabbatical leave, I was able to assign as many footnotes to the text as possible. Mr. Krohn had a system whereby each page was given a letter indicating the draft: "a" = first draft, "b" = second draft, etc. Some versions of the footnotes included a word or phrase in the text which further aided my task, and sometimes previous versions of chapters provided clues. The following summary will indicate the problems and solutions:

chapter

1 31 footnotes not used; the information in the 95 that remain are combined to 52.

2 7 footnotes not used.

3 Footnotes 72-135 were undoubtedly intended for use in his larger unpublished study on Nathaniel Phillips cited in the quote above.

5 6 additional footnotes refer to copies in the Gaylord Music Library.

6 10 unused footnotes refer to Krohn's own *Missouri Music.*

8   Three sets of footnotes, on three separate pages and all different in content, are not used.

9   I assigned three footnotes, originally numbered 227-29 (!), but was unable to use those numbered 230-58, which must have been intended for another study.

10   There are 28 unused footnotes, of which I could assign only numbers 1-10; almost all cite copies of music in the Gaylord Music Library, the number of plates, and plate numbers.

11   I was unable to assign the 23 footnotes; most of them refer to the Sonneck and Muller books mentioned in the substitute Reference note.

12   Nine footnote numbers--only five of them filled in, are represented in the References list.

17   The Reference list substitutes for 15 footnotes, all to the same source.

18   I was able to assign only two footnotes; 31 additional ones all cite copies of music in the Gaylord Music Library.

20   I was unable to assign 19 additional footnotes; 17 of them refer to copies in the Gaylord Music Library.

All other references in the typescript are present in this volume.

Mrs. Krause performed a major contribution towards this publication in checking for accuracy many details of titles, composers, spelling, and dates, with the original sheet music in Mr. Krohn's collection. Dr. Donald Krummel, University of Illinois, Urbana-Champaign, and Dr. Richard Wetzel, Ohio University, kindly read the manuscript and made a number of suggestions which have been incorporated. Extensive revision and rewriting were also suggested, but Mr. Krohn had stated before he died that he did not wish anything changed. Therefore, what appears here represents pretty much what he left.

In early 1987 I put this book on my home computer (program: Nota Bene), and the results were printed at the University of Kansas word processing office through the courtesy of Nancy Kreighbaum and Paula Malone. James R. Heintze, who succeeded my wife and I as series editor for Bibliographies in American Music in 1985, found some additional information at the Library of Congress. Susanne Bell, Mrs. Krause's successor as librarian at the Gaylord Music Library, kindly made available the plates of illustrative material included here.

In the final stages, George R. Keck, of Ouachita Baptist University, Arkadelphia, Arkansas, with the background of his 2-volume 1982 University of Iowa dissertation "Pre-1875 American Imprint Sheet Music in the Ernst C. Krohn Special Collection, Gaylord Music Library, Washington University, St. Louis, Missouri: A Catalog and Descriptive Study," kindly read through this book, correcting further errors and adding location information at the Gaylord Music Library for pre-1875 items. In a letter, he explained: "Krohn divided his collection between Gaylord, St. Louis University, Webster College, and the Priory in St. Louis County; thus many of the imprints that he indicated as part of his collection are now in Gaylord. Many others are not. That also is the case with the collection of Harold Linebeck, and many of the imprints indicated by Krohn as in Linebeck's collection are now in Gaylord."

Further tribute comes from another important researcher into earlier American music, H. Earle Johnson, now of Williamsburg, Virginia. In July 1981, he wrote this about Krohn:

> Dear Ernst! In 1946 I visited him in St. Louis. At that time his was the largest musicological library west of the Mississippi (I believe). Anyway, it was very large and notable for scholarly German works. He wasn't young then, but we hit

it off very well. He and his sister entertained me very graciously. Krohn was lonesome as a scholar--he had never been east of the Mississippi, I believe; thereafter we corresponded into the 1970s when he moved to New Mexico. He was a real beaver insofar as research is concerned, a real Germanophile, particularly devoted to the history of music in St. Louis. As we know, a distinguished lot of German émigrées came there from 1848 on; they were intensely musical and he was born into that musically romantic atmosphere. It was a pleasure to know such a warm-hearted, gentle man.

I am sorry never to have had the pleasure of meeting Mr. Krohn, who had become a legend in his own day. His research into music in Missouri represents a lifetime's work, and he was a primary witness to over a half-century of it, as evidenced in chapter 16 and the first footnote of chapter 19. The publication of this book on the occasion of the centennial of his birth is intended to honor him. May his pioneering interest and enthusiasm for music of his own region provide an example for the rest of us.

J. Bunker Clark
University of Kansas
February 1988

MUSIC PUBLISHING IN ST. LOUIS

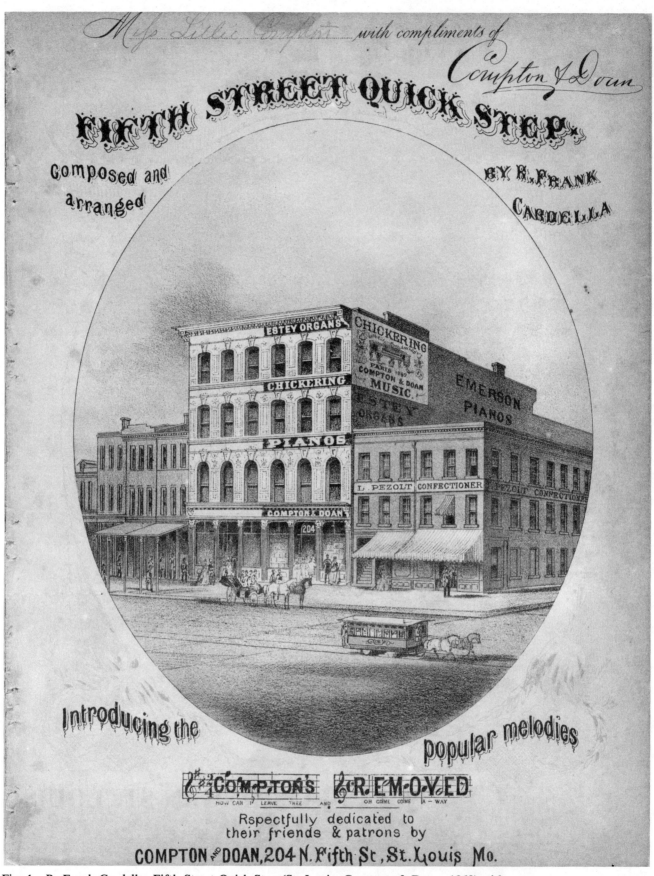

Fig. 1. R. Frank Cardella, Fifth Street Quick Step (St. Louis: Compton & Doan, 1868), title-page

1

PROLOGUE

It must not be forgotten that the discovery of a New World by a navigator of Spanish derivation did not generate any specific amount of enthusiasm for exploration at the French court. Francis I, King of France, was too busy with his Italian wars to take much interest in trans-Atlantic adventure.[1] The return to Seville in 1522 of the *Victoria*, the last of the caravels of Magellan, brought the matter forcibly to his attention. He reacted in 1523 by engaging Giovanni da Verrazzano, the Florentine mariner, to sail to the new continent.[2] In his sturdy vessel *La Dauphine*, Verrazzano in 1524 cruised along the American coast from Georgia to Maine, and upon his return to France he submitted a brilliantly descriptive narrative of his voyage.[3]

Ten years later, the king outfitted Jacques Cartier,[4] an experienced French pilot, with two small ships whose names we do not know, to explore the Gulf of St. Lawrence. The next year Cartier was put in charge of three vessels, *La Grande Hermine* (his flagship) and two smaller boats, *La Petite Hermine* and *L'Esmerillon*.[5] He returned to the Gulf of the St. Lawrence and entered the St. Lawrence River. He ascended its vast channel until he reached Hochelaga, the site of the future Montreal. On the way back he stopped at Stadconé, the site of Quebec, where he spent a miserable winter.[6]

This was not the first French contact with the New World. Before John Cabot's discovery of the Grand Banks of Newfoundland in 1497, French and Portuguese fishermen had fished in its waters, the French as early as 1504.[7] But fishermen are not explorers and leave no written records. Samuel Champlain, intrepid explorer, actually founded a permanent settlement at

---

1. L. P. Kellogg, *The French Regime in Wisconsin and the Northwest* (Madison, 1925; reprint, New York: Cooper Square, 1968), 8.

2. J. R. Hale, *The Age of Exploration* (New York), 99-101; Kellogg, 9-14.

3. Kellogg, 10, 14; S. E. Morison, *The European Discovery of America* (New York, 1971), 277-325; L. C. Wroth, *The Voyages of Giovanni Verrazano* (New York, 1970).

4. Morison, 339-87; Kellogg, 15-17; Hale, 101.

5. Y. F. Zoltvany, comp., *The French Tradition in America* (Columbia, 1969), 33-36; Morison, 388-429; Kellogg, 17-19; Hale, 101.

6. B. Keating, *The Grand Banks* (New York, 1968), 32-34; F. Parkman, *Pioneers of France in the New World* (1865; reprint, Williamstown, Mass.: Corner House, 1970), 191-93; Morison, 178-79, 225, 270-74, 470, 491; Kellogg, 8; Hale, 100.

7. *Dictionary of American Biography* (henceforth, DAB), ed. Allen Johnson and Dumas Malone, 20 vols. (New York, 1928-37), 3:605-06; Kellogg, 44-64; Parkman, 185-87, 189-464.

Quebec in 1608. He ventured further west in 1615 and discovered Lake Ontario. Lake Huron had been discovered by Father Le Caron a short time before.[8]

Samuel Champlain had died 25 December 1635, but his exploratory work had been carried on by his associates, particularly Jean Nicolet,[9] who discovered Lake Michigan and set foot on the future state of Wisconsin. Lake Superior seems to have been discovered by Champlain's interpreter Étienne Brulé, accompanied by a companion, Grenoble. The last of the Great Lakes to be discovered was Lake Erie.[10] A group of Jesuits explored its shores, intending to found a mission, but failed to find a suitable site.

In 1673, Louis Joliet, a Canadian surveyor, and the scholarly Jesuit Father Jacques Marquette, traversed the Illinois River until its junction with the Mississippi.[11] They paddled down the broad expanse of the Father of Waters until they reached the mouth of the Arkansas River where they concluded to return to Canada. Only Joliet reached Quebec, for Father Marquette died on the shore of Lake Michigan, 19 May 1675.[12]

The French explorer Daniel Greysolon, Sieur Duluth,[13] achieved the distinction of penetrating furthest west. While negotiating a treaty of peace with the Sioux Indians in 1679, he took possession of the country in the name of the King of France and affixed the royal arms to a majestic oak tree near Mille Lacs Lake in what is now Minnesota.[14] The upper basin of the Mississippi was extensively explored by the Franciscan Recollect friar Father Louis Hennepin, who also published the first drawing of Niagara Falls in 1683.

René Robert Cavelier, Sieur de la Salle, and his faithful companion Henry Tonty, in 1682, canoed all the way down the Mississippi to the Gulf of Mexico.[15] While at the Gulf, La Salle took formal possession of the future Louisiana in the name of the King of France. In the course of his expedition he also founded several forts, notably Fort Prudhomme on the Mississippi in 1682 and Fort St. Louis on the Illinois River in 1683.[16]

---

8. Parkman, 405, 411; Kellogg, 54-55.

9. Kellogg, 63-83; Zoltvany, 36-42; Parkman, 456-64; J. P. Caruso, *The Mississippi Valley Frontier* (New York, 1966), 115-21; DAB 13:511.

10. Kellogg, 59-60, 86-87.

11. Kellogg, 191-201; Caruso, 149-57; DAB 10:156-57; F. A. Ogg, *The Opening of the Mississippi* (Bloomington, 1904; reprint, New York: Cooper Square, 1969), 65-80; E. Kenton, *Jesuit Relations and Allied Documents* (New York, 1954), 333-75; J. P. Donnelley, *James Marquette, S.J.* (Chicago, 1968).

12. Kellogg, 168; Kenton, 376-87; Caruso, 157; Donnelley, 252-66.

13. DAB 5:500-01; Kellogg, 207-14; Ogg, 138-43.

14. Ogg, 139-40; Kellogg, 210 (particularly the map, but note that Mille Lacs Lake is in Minnesota and is not to be confused with Lac des Milles which is in Ontario and north of Lake Superior).

15. Ogg, 81-132; Caruso, 159-81; DAB 11:10-12; DAB 18:587-88; J. U. Terrell, *La Salle* (New York, 1968), 101-02. Terrell (pp. 47-48) claims that La Salle, in 1671, preceded Joliet and Marquette in the discovery of the Mississippi; this cannot be substantiated.

16. S. Wilson, "Colonial Fortifications and Military Architecture in the Mississippi Valley," in *The French in the Mississippi Valley*, ed. F. J. McDermott (Urbana, 1965), 103-22; the map "French Mississippi-Missouri Exploration 1673-1750" in *American Heritage Pictorial Atlas of United States History* (New York, 1966), 53; Caruso, 176, 179-80; Kellogg, 224, fn. 3.

The French voyageurs, *coureurs de bois*, and the missionaries who explored the vast reaches of the upper Mississippi valley during the seventeenth and eighteenth centuries, achieved far more than they realized.[17] Their immediate motivation was the satisfaction derived from penetrating the limitless unknown. The priests hoped to find new souls to save; the *coureurs de bois* and *voyageurs* were forever searching for unknown rendezvous of fur-bearing creatures. What they actually accomplished was to prepare the way for the introduction of a French culture that soon pervaded the entire valley, but struck roots more deeply in the south than in the west.

The Seminary Fathers of Quebec, in 1699, established the Mission of the Holy Family of the Tamaroas, which became the core of the future village of Cahokia.[18] This proved to be the first French settlement in the Illinois country,[19] and was located across the river from St. Louis. At the mouth of the River des Pères, there existed a French Jesuit mission and a village from the fall of 1700 to the spring of 1703. This was the first French settlement in Missouri. In the summer of 1703, the priest of this Des Pères post, Father Pierre Gabriel Marest, led his flock across the Mississippi to the Kaskaskia River where he founded the Mission of Notre Dame of the Cascasquois, which eventually became the village of Kaskaskia.[20]

The struggle for supremacy in the New World between France and England came to a dramatic end at Quebec in 1759. The sanguinary conflict on the Plains of Abraham, the death of both generals James Wolfe and the Marquis of Montcalm, the decisive defeat of the French, all transpired in the relatively few hours on that tragic Thursday morning the thirteenth of September. The power of France in North America was definitely broken. The treaty of Paris negotiated in February of 1763 awarded to England practically all of the country east of the Mississippi River. In a secret treaty signed at Fontainebleau, 3 November 1762, France ceded to Spain her vast Louisiana Territory that comprised all of the land west of the Mississippi River. Spain did not assert her sovereignty immediately, so that for several years many of the French inhabitants continued to think of themselves as subjects of the French crown.

The lower valley was first penetrated by the Spaniards, whose all-pervading purpose was to find gold. The lower Mississippi River was discovered by the Spanish explorer Hernando de Soto,[21] who on 8 May 1541 rather accidentally stumbled upon the river at some point below the future Memphis. A year later, 21 May 1542, he died and was buried in the river he was trying to explore.

Coming directly from France, Pierre Lemoyne, Sieur d'Iberville, and his eighteen-year-old brother Jean Baptiste, discovered the mouth of the Mississippi, 2 March 1699, and ascended

---

17. Caruso, 115-16; Ogg, 133-38.

18. N. Baillargeon, "The Seminary of Quebec," in *The French in the Mississippi Valley*, 197-202; Zoltvany, 75-78; A. B. Seuss, *The Romantic Story of Cahokia* (Belleville, 1943; 2nd ed., 1947), 12-14, 49-51; J. C. Wild, *The Valley of the Mississippi* (St. Louis, 1841; reprint, St. Louis: J. Garnier, 1946), 103-06; Caruso, 251; E. D. Fite and A. Freeman, *A Book of Old Maps* (Cambridge, 1926; reprint, New York: Dover, 1969), 278-81.

19. G. J. Garraghan, "Earliest Settlements of the Illinois Country," *Catholic Historical Review* 15 (January 1930): 355; C. W. Alvord, *The Illinois Country*, The Centennial History of Illinois, 1 (Springfield, 1920; reprint, Chicago: Loyola Press, 1965).

20. L. Houck, *A History of Missouri*, 3 vols. (Chicago, 1908; reprint, New York: Arno, 1971), 1:242-43; Garraghan, 357-59; J. F. Bannon, S.J., "Black-Robe Frontiersman: Gabriel Marest," *Bulletin of the Missouri Historical Society* 10 (April 1954): 351-66; DAB 12:280-81; Caruso, 252, 328-32; Wild, 61-66; Fite and Freeman, 279-80; Ogg, 219; Alvord, 153, 236-38; *The French in the Mississippi Valley*, 119.

21. Ogg, 28-40; Kellogg, 26-28; DAB 5:256-58.

the river for an uncertain distance. They returned to the Gulf and founded Fort Maurepas at the head of Biloxi Bay in April of the same year. The following year d'Iberville ascended the Mississippi and erected Fort Boulaye on a bluff fifty miles above the mouth of the river.[22] This was the first settlement in the present state of Louisiana. A geologist with d'Iberville's company, Pierre Charles le Seuer, provided with a license to operate copper mines in the upper Mississippi valley, travelled up the river, built Fort l'Hullier on the Minnesota River, attempted to mine (but unsuccessfully), and returned to Fort Maurepas in 1702. It was not until 1739 that Louis Denis, Sieur de la Ronde, succeeded in working the copper mines on Lake Superior.[23]

D'Iberville died of yellow fever at Havana, 9 July 1706.[24] The brother of d'Iberville, Jean Baptiste Lemoyne, Sieur de Bienville, with headquarters at Fort St. Louis on the Mobile River, was in reality the first French governor of Louisiana.[25] He was recalled to France for alleged irregularities in 1708, but could not leave until 1713, at which time he was supplanted by Antoine de la Mothe Cadillac, who had founded Detroit in 1701.[26] Cadillac was recalled in 1716,[27] and Bienville was returned to power. The same year he ascended the Mississippi and built Fort Rosalie on the high bluffs that eventually became the site of the town of Natchez.[28] Two years later he founded the trading post on a curve in the river that soon became the thriving village of New Orleans.[29] In 1722 he made it the capital of the territory of Louisiana.

The residents of New Orleans organized a rebellion against the cession and it was not until Count Alexander O'Reilly, Lieutenant-General of the armies of Spain, appeared before New Orleans on 18 August 1769, with twenty-five ships loaded with Spanish troops, that the recalcitrant citizens capitulated. General O'Reilly started his career as Spanish governor of Louisiana by having five of the leaders of the rebellion shot.[30] They were Pierre Caresse, Nicholas Chauvin de Lefreniere, Pierre Marquis, Joseph Milhet, Jean Baptist Noyan, all five of them martyrs to the cause of self-determination.

A year later, O'Reilly fell into disgrace and was recalled to Spain. He was succeeded by Don Luis de Unzaga y Anerzaga who functioned as governor from 1770 to 1777.[31] The governor next in line was Don Bernardo de Galvez who won fame in the war with England and remained active practically until his death in Mexico, 30 November 1786.[32] In 1783-84 he had

---

22. DAB 9:455-57; Caruso, 225-40; Ogg, 174-86; *The French in the Mississippi Valley*, 107-10, 116.

23. Caruso, 241-48; Ogg, 164-66; Kellogg, 274-75, 351-57; DAB 11:191-92.

24. Ogg, 190; DAB 9:456.

25. Caruso, 229-40; Ogg, 178-87, 192-95; DAB 2:250-52; *The French in the Mississippi Valley*, 110-11.

26. Ogg, 196, fn. 3, 198; Caruso, 257; DAB 3:397-98.

27. Caruso, 259; Ogg, 203.

28. J. Daniels, *The Devil's Backbone* (New York, 1962), 12-14.

29. *The French in the Mississippi Valley*, 111-12; C. Gayarre, *History of Louisiana*, 4 vols. (New Orleans, 1885), 1:234-36; *United States Encyclopedia of History*, 16 vols. (New York, 1967-68), 12:225-60; Ogg, 208-11, 220-24, 228.

30. Ogg, 320-41; H. Carter, *Man and the River* (Chicago, 1970), 48.

31. Ogg, 341, 367; Caruso, 333.

32. Caruso, 338-39; Ogg, 367-72; DAB 7:119-20.

visited Madrid, at which time he was appointed Captain General of Louisiana and the Floridas, and in 1785 he was made Viceroy of New Spain. His successor, Don Estevan Miro, had been in command while he was in Spain and Cuba.[33] Miro returned to Spain in 1791, when he was made Brigadier General and finally Lieutenant General. The last Spanish governor was the Baron Francisco Luis Hector Carondelet[34] who served until 1797 when he was made Governor General of Quito, capital of Colombia.

Meanwhile, Gilbert Antoine de St. Maxent, a wealthy merchant in New Orleans, and Pierre Laclede Liguest, an adventurer, joined forces to promote trade with the Indians of the upper Mississippi valley. Chevalier de Kerlerec, French governor of Louisiana, granted them a license for that purpose in 1762. Their association was known as Maxent, Laclede & Company, also as the Louisiana Fur Company; an expedition was outfitted and under the leadership of Laclede proceeded up the river.[35]

After three months of arduous river travel it reached Ste. Genevieve only to find that the accommodations were inadequate.[36] The commandant at Fort Chartres, Chevalier Joseph Pierre de Noyon de Villiers, offered Laclede adequate storage space for his supplies and satisfactory quarters for his personnel, which Laclede accepted. A not inconsiderable part of Laclede's party consisted of Laclede's civil-law wife, Madame Maria Thérèse Chouteau, and her five children.[37] Laclede found a suitable location for his trading post on the west bank of the river. On 14 February 1764, he sent his fourteen-year-old stepson René Auguste Chouteau with thirty French Canadians from Kaskaskia to build cabins in the area of the future St. Louis.[38] The new trading post thrived unexpectedly, thanks to its excellent location, and by 1774 had six hundred and fifty inhabitants.[39] As a result of the secret treaty of 1762, St. Louis finally acquired a Spanish governor in 1770, Don Pedro José de Piernas,[40] who was actually Lieutenant-Governor of Upper Louisiana. In 1775 he was succeeded by Don Francesco Cruzat, who was replaced by Don Fernando de Leyba in 1778, but Cruzat returned to power when Leyba died in 1780.[41] Cruzat was succeeded by Don Manuel Perez in 1787, who in turn was

---

33. Houck, 2:122-29, fn. 9.

34. Houck, 1:323-32, 2:170, 176; Ogg, 450-51; DAB 3:507-08.

35. Houck, 2:1, fn. 2, 2-4; Caruso, 327-32; DAB 10:520-21; J. F. McDermott, "Myths and Realities Concerning the Founding of St. Louis," in *The French in the Mississippi Valley*, 1-15; Ogg, 663.

36. Caruso, 328; Houck, 2:4-5; McDermott, "Myths and Realities," 9.

37. Houck, 2:4, fn. 11.

38. Houck, 2:1-9; Caruso, 328-29; DAB 4:94-95; McDermott, "Myths and Realities," 8-10; A. Chouteau, "Narrative of the Settlement of St. Louis," in *The Early Histories of St. Louis*, ed. J. F. McDermott (St. Louis, 1952), 47-49.

39. L. Houck, *The Spanish Regime in Missouri*, 2 vols. (Chicago, 1909), 1:61.

40. Houck, *Spanish Regime*, 1:xxiii-xix; Houck, *History of Missouri*, 1:296-302 and 2:29-30; Caruso, 333-36.

41. Caruso, 336-50; Houck, *Spanish Regime*, 1:xix-xxi; Houck, *History of Missouri*, 1:303-11 and 2:30-51.

replaced by Don Zenon Trudeau in 1792.[42] By 1799, Don Carlos de Hault de Lassus became Lieutenant-Governor, but Spanish dominion ceased in 1800 and Louisiana returned to French ownership.[43] The Louisiana Purchase ended that, and on 4 March 1804 Captain Amos Stoddard of the United States Army formally transferred Louisiana from Spain to France and from France to the United States.[44]

During all this time St. Louis had flourished as a French community that by 1799 had over nine hundred inhabitants. The four Spaniards who had strayed in our midst married French wives and raised French families.[45] Due to its development as a center of commerce, St. Louis attracted men of superior education and intellectual ability. It did not have a newspaper nor was there much literary activity. Since the emphasis was on commerce, there was no need of philosophic or religious discussion. That the citizens of St. Louis were well-read is evidenced by the fact that John Francis McDermott could compile a book recording the titles of approximately three thousand books that could be found, in his *Private Libraries in Creole Saint Louis*.[46] When Laclede died in 1778, he left a library of two hundred volumes. Antoine François Saugrain, who was surgeon at Fort Bellefontaine, left a library of three hundred and fifty books in 1820. Auguste Chouteau collected a library of over six hundred volumes, of which some were sold and some retained by his widow, Madame Thérèse Cerré Chouteau, upon his death in 1829. Some two hundred stockholders organized a subscription library that possessed over a thousand books in 1825. The library of St. Louis University accumulated a collection of over five thousand titles by 1842.[47] A printed catalog as of 1842 is currently available at St. Louis University.

An Irishman, Joseph Charless,[48] late of Louisville, set up the first printing press in St. Louis, and started to publish the weekly *Missouri Gazette* in 1808.[49] He undoubtedly did some

---

42. Houck, *History of Missouri*, 1:312-15, 318-32, 2:52-62; Houck, *Spanish Regime*, l:xxi-xxiv; J. Lecompte, "Don Benito Vasquez in Early St. Louis," *Bulletin of the Missouri Historical Society* 26 (July 1970): 300-01.

43. Houck, *History of Missouri*, 1:332-36, 2:62; Houck, *Spanish Regime*, l:xxiv; Lecompte, 302-03.; Caruso, 355; Ogg, 463-67, 473-77.

44. Houck, *History of Missouri*, 2:355-75, 3:160-61; Caruso, 355; Ogg, 495-538. For an amusing description of the discussion of the Louisiana Purchase between Napoleon and his two brothers, Lucien and Joseph, while Bonaparte was taking a bath, see Ogg, 523-28.

45. Houck, *History of Missouri* 2:209, 286; Lecompte, 297.

46. J. F. McDermott, *Private Libraries in Creole Saint Louis* (Baltimore, 1938), 16-18. By contrast, New Orleans had its first French newspaper, the weekly *Moniteur de la Louisiana*, from 1794 to 1814. A second bilingual paper, the semi-weekly *Le Telegraphe, et le Commercial Advertiser*, appeared from 1803 to 1812. An English weekly, *The Union or New Orleans Advertiser*, began its career in 1803; the *Orleans Gazette* in 1804. See C. S. Brigham, *History and Bibliography of American Newspapers, 1690-1820*, 2 vols. (Worcester, 1947), 1:189-92; also J. C. Oswald, *Printing in the Americas* (New York, 1937; Kennicat reprint, 1965), 302-04.

47. McDermott, *Private Libraries*, 19-20, 26-43, 90-107, 128,66, 173-76; Houck, *History of Missouri*, 3:72.

48. W. H. Lyon, "Joseph Charless, Father of Missouri Journalism," *Bulletin of the Missouri Historical Society* 17 (January 1961): 133-45; R. L. Rusk, *Literature of the Middle Western Frontier*, 2 vols. (New York, 1926), 1:139-40; DAB 4:23.

49. Brigham, 1:433-34; Oswald, 354-57.

job printing and by 1809 had turned out two books. *An Oration Delivered before Saint Louis Lodge No. 111 at the Town of Saint Louis in the Territory of Louisiana, the 9th Day of November, 1808 . . .* by Frederic Bates bears the date 1809 and may be the first book printed in Missouri.[50] *The Laws of the Territory of Missouri*, a massive volume of 436 pages, bears the imprint 1808, but must have been printed in 1809, for on page 373 it has the printed certificate of Frederic Bates, dated 29 April 1809.

The *Missouri Gazette* flourished although it changed its name several times. Eventually, under the ownership of Edward Charless, the son of Joseph, the *Gazette* became the *Missouri Republican*, which in 1835 became a daily paper. Actually, the first daily paper was the *Herald*, started in 1834 by Treadway and Holbrook, but it soon expired. Meanwhile, a rival of the *Gazette* put in its appearance when Joseph Norvell of Nashville issued the first number of the *Western Journal* in 1815. Two years later it changed ownership and became *The Western Emigrant*, only to blossom forth as *The St. Louis Enquirer* in 1818. By 1827, its name was transformed into *The Beacon*. A descendant of this family of papers flourished from 1835 to 1841 as *The Argus*.[51] The first German paper *Der Anzeiger des Westens* began its career in 1835. It was not until 1855 that the French weekly *La Revue l'Oest*, edited by Louis Richard Cortambert, appeared. It was short-lived, for it expired in about 1858.[52]

---

50. Thomas W. Streeter, supplement to Roy T. King, "The Territorial Press in Missouri," *Bulletin of the Missouri Historical Society* 11 (January 1955): 202-03; V. A. Perotti, *Important Firsts in Missouri Imprints, 1808-1858* (Kansas City, 1967), 1-4; Oswald, 353-56.

51. Oswald, 355-58; Brigham, 1:432.

52. D. Kaser, *Directory of the St. Louis Book and Printing Trades* (New York, 1961), 15; A. N. DeMenil, *The Literature of the Louisiana Territory* (St. Louis, 1904), 46.

2

THE PIONEERS

In the words of John Francis McDermott, "everybody sold books in early St. Louis."[1] Jacob Philipson, late of Philadelphia, opened a general store in 1808. In the 10 November 1808 issue of the *Missouri Gazette* he announced that he had "a few German and English Bibles and Testaments, Hymn Books, etc., for sale."[2] Joseph Charless, editor and publisher of the *Gazette*, in the issue of 9 November 1809, offered for sale *The Lexington Collection, Being a Selection of Hymns and Spiritual Songs*.[3] This collection was probably identical with a *Selection of Hymns and Spiritual Songs*, printed while Charless was publisher of the *Independent Gazeteer* at Lexington, Kentucky, early in 1803. He still had copies for sale in 1812.

Even the drugstores sold books. Simpson & Quarles, druggists, advertised on 20 June 1816 their stock of drugs as well as a "handsome selection of school and miscellaneous books." On 17 October 1817 they offered for sale "*The Columbian Harmonist*, a selection of Sacred Music on a new and improved plan."[4] This psalmtune book was compiled by Timothy Flint, the itinerant preacher,[5] and published at Cincinnati in 1816. Dr. Arthur Nelson advertised on 19 May 1818 that he had for sale at his drugstore "French, Spanish, and English, Classical and School Books--Music Assorted."[6] It would be fascinating to know what Dr. Nelson had in mind when he offered "Music Assorted."

The general dealers Sanguinette & Bright announced 2 April 1818 that they had received from New Orleans "Books, French and English."[7] Bernard Gilhuly and James Cummins, on 29 March 1820, announced the arrival from New York, via New Orleans, of an "invoice of Religious, Scientific, Classical and School Books, in French and English." J. P. Lacroze & Company, "Confectionery and Cordial Distillers," advertised 4 April 1821 that they had "books to be raffled for." The auctioneer Thomas F. Riddick announced on 5 April 1820 that he had just received a lot of books that he would sell for cash. Many of the fine French libraries were sold by auction. Since people expected to pick up bargains at an auction sale, the auctioneer livened

---

1. J. F. McDermott, "Everybody Sold Books in Early St. Louis," *Publishers' Weekly* 132 (1937): 248-50.

2. McDermott, 248; also E. C. Krohn, "The Philipsons, the First Jewish Family in St. Louis and Their Impact on Art and Music" (unpublished; at Gaylord Music Library).

3. E. C. Krohn, "The Missouri Harmony," *Bulletin of the Missouri Historical Society* 6 (October 1949): 25. Reprinted in *Missouri Music*, 189.

4. McDermott, 249.

5. F. J. Metcalf, *American Psalmody* (New York, 1917; reprint, New York: Da Capo, 1968), 23.

6. McDermott, 249.

7. McDermott, 248.

up a dull season by buying books in the East and selling them here at a fraudulent auction sale.[8] The traffic in books was increasing in volume so that a book store would have to turn up.

In 1820, Thomas Essex and Charles Beynroth opened the first book shop at the Sign of the Ledger on Main Street, "next door to Mr. Savage's store."[9] In 1821 the store was located at 60 North Main Street, but the proprietors were now Thomas Essex and Daniel Hough.[10] The shop was still at the same spot in 1826, but now Thomas Houghan was the partner of Essex. In 1827 Thomas Essex opened the St. Louis Bookstore "next door to H. C. Simmons and Company," while Thomas Houghan carried on alone at 60 Main Street until 1832.[11] Meanwhile, George Holton opened a bookstore on Main Street in 1830, James C. Essex at 61 North Main Street in 1832, and in the same year Stephen W. Meech established the Franklin Bookstore on "Main street, a few doors above the bank."[12]

The *Missouri Gazette*, in the issues of 31 May and 7 June 1820, contained an advertisement of "Vocal Music Books, *The Missouri Harmony* just published and for sale at the bookstore of Mr. Essex."[13] This historically very important book was printed in Cincinnati but it bore a St. Louis imprint and was apparently compiled by Allen D. Carden for use in the "School for Teaching the Theory and Practice of Vocal Music," which he announced in the same issues of the *Gazette*.[14] The 200-page psalm book was printed in the customary oblong format and the tunes were harmonized and typeset in the usual *fasola* shape-note notation.[15] The title-page is quite informative (see Fig. 2). Only eighty-six copies seem to have survived.[16]

Far more scarce is *The St. Louis Harmony*, published at Cincinnati in 1831 (see Fig. 3).[17] The only surviving copy seems to be the one picked up at an auction sale in the Ozark country

---

8. McDermott, 248-50.

9. McDermott, "The First Bookstore in St. Louis," *Mid-America* 21 (1939): 206-08; D. Kaser, *A Directory of the St. Louis Book and Printing Trades to 1850* (New York, 1961), 20.

10. Kaser, 20; McDermott, "First Bookstore," 206-08.

11. Kaser, 24, 31.

12. Kaser, 23, 20, 21, 27.

13. See Krohn, *A Century of Missouri Music* (St. Louis, 1924; reprint, New York: Da Capo, 1970), 5.

14. Krohn, 5.

15. See Krohn, "Missouri Harmony," 25-33 (*Missouri Music*, 189-97). Copies are in the Missouri Historical Society and in the library of E. C. Krohn. [Krohn's library is now at the Gaylord Music Library, Washington University. According to Richard J. Stanislaw, *A Checklist of Four-Shape Shape-Note Tunebooks*, I.S.A.M. Monographs, 10 (Brooklyn: Institute for Studies in American Music, Brooklyn College, CUNY, 1978), item 8, there are also copies at the Library of Congress, Boston Public Library, University of Michigan Clements Library, University of Missouri-Kansas City Conservatory of Music, and the Ladies' Hermitage Association in Hermitage, Tennessee. See also Shirley Ann Bean, "*The Missouri Harmony*, 1820-1858: The Refinement of a Southern Tunebook" (D.M.A. dissertation, University of Missouri-Kansas City, 1973). —Ed.]

16. See Krohn, "A Check List of Editions of 'The Missouri Harmony'," *Bulletin of the Missouri Historical Society* 6 (April 1950): 375, and the facsimile of the title-page on p. 377. (Reprinted in *Missouri Music*, 201, 203.)

17. Copy at the Missouri Historical Society.

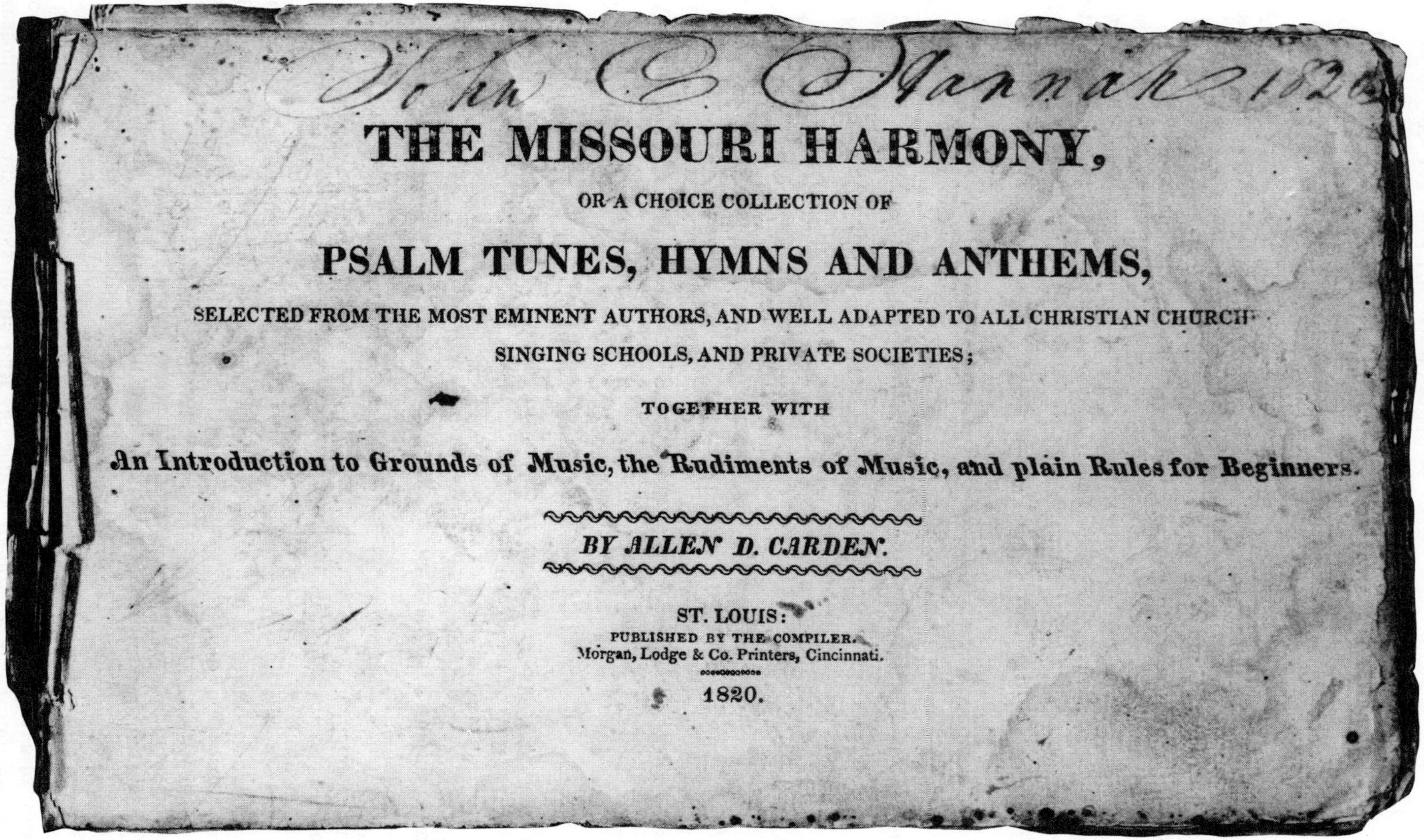
John C. Hannah 1820
THE MISSOURI HARMONY,
OR A CHOICE COLLECTION OF
PSALM TUNES, HYMNS AND ANTHEMS,
SELECTED FROM THE MOST EMINENT AUTHORS, AND WELL ADAPTED TO ALL CHRISTIAN CHURCH
SINGING SCHOOLS, AND PRIVATE SOCIETIES;
TOGETHER WITH
An Introduction to Grounds of Music, the Rudiments of Music, and plain Rules for Beginners.
BY ALLEN D. CARDEN.
ST. LOUIS:
PUBLISHED BY THE COMPILER.
Morgan, Lodge & Co. Printers, Cincinnati.
1820.

Fig. 2. Allan D. Carden, *The Missouri Harmony* (St. Louis: Carden, 1820), title-page

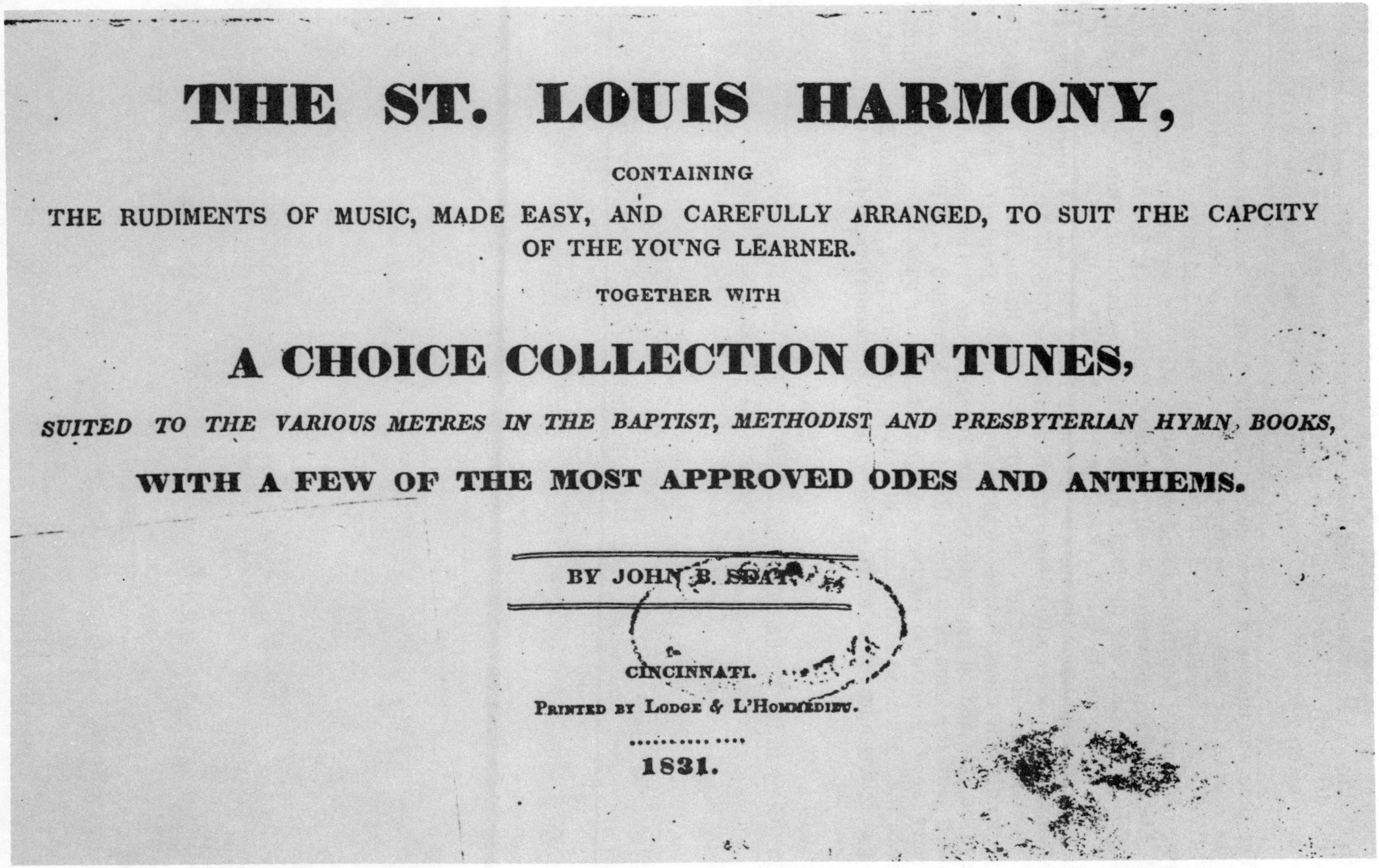

THE ST. LOUIS HARMONY,

CONTAINING

THE RUDIMENTS OF MUSIC, MADE EASY, AND CAREFULLY ARRANGED, TO SUIT THE CAPCITY OF THE YOUNG LEARNER.

TOGETHER WITH

A CHOICE COLLECTION OF TUNES,

SUITED TO THE VARIOUS METRES IN THE BAPTIST, METHODIST AND PRESBYTERIAN HYMN BOOKS,

WITH A FEW OF THE MOST APPROVED ODES AND ANTHEMS.

BY JOHN B. SEAT.

CINCINNATI.

PRINTED BY LODGE & L'HOMMEDIEU.

....

1831.

Fig. 3. John B. Seat, *The St. Louis Harmony* (Cincinnati: Lodge & L'Hommedieu, 1831), title-page

by Charles van Ravenswaay in 1952. An advertisement in the *St. Louis Times* on the 8th and the 16th of July, 1831, mentions *Kirkham's Grammar*[18] and the *Missouri Harmony* offered for sale at the drugstore of George Holton at Main and Market. The *St. Louis Harmony* was undoubtedly offered for sale in St. Louis, but no advertisement has come to light revealing that fact.

The time was ripe for a music store. That it was on its way may be inferred from several ads in the *Beacon* for 1830. In the June 17 issue there appeared a very informative advertisement: "MUSIC--For the Piano Forte, Flute, Violin, Guitar, and Harp. An excellent assortment, consisting of Sonatas, Sonatinas, Rondos, Waltzes, Marches, variations, &c., &c." composed by "Pleyel, Stiebett [*sic*], Schmidt, Woelfl, Cramer, Reotti [*sic*], Beethoven, &c., &c.,--Also-- INSTRUCTION BOOKS, for the Piano Forte, Flageolet, Clarionet, Flute, Violin, and Harp, for sale at a very low price, by G. CLARKE, of the Theatre." Could this be the same Clarke who acted in several plays during the summer season of 1830? This ad was repeated July 29.

Meanwhile, another advertisement appeared in the *Beacon*, 24 June 1830. It ran: "NEW MUSIC: a choice selection of new and admired English, Italian, and French Songs, Ballads and Duetts; splendid Variations, Rondos, Waltzes, Marches, Quick Steps, etc., arranged for Piano and Flute can be obtained on application at the *Beacon* office." The readers of the *Beacon* were confronted with the same ad in the issue of July 22, coupled with the surprising information that prices were reduced to twelve and a half cents per page. The same information was brought to their attention in the issues of July 29, August 5, 12, 19, and 26. Neither of these attempts at selling music seem to have met with much encouragement from the public.

---

18. Copy in the Krohn collection.

3

NATHANIEL PHILLIPS

It all happened when I came across a fragile piece of paper upon which was imprinted a list of some of the publications of Nathaniel Phillips, presumably the first music publisher in St. Louis. These were the pre-xerox days when I could not have a copy made immediately of my precious find. When I next visited the venerable library of the Missouri Historical Society, prepared to make a copy of my rare sheet, I was completely dismayed to find that it had vanished into thin air. Nor has it turned up since. Somehow or other that slight incident stimulated in me an abiding interest in the work of Nathaniel Phillips.

An advertisement in the *Missouri Republican* for 22 December 1837 announced "A NEW ESTABLISHMENT, Natha'l Phillips, Umbrella and Parasol Manufacturer, No. 28 Market street, three doors from the Museum,[1] where he manufactures and keeps constantly on hand, Umbrellas, Whips, Parasols, Dentists Instruments, Billiard Balls, Canes, etc. Musical Instruments, Whips, and Umbrellas repaired."[2] On 7 January 1838, the *Missouri Republican* could publish

> A CARD: N. Phillips having had several requests to establish a Music Store in St. Louis, has concluded to devote his time to that business. He has just returned from the eastern cities, where he has selected a large and valuable assortment of MUSIC, MUSICAL INSTRUMENTS and MUSICAL MERCHANDISE of every variety and of the best quality. Also a large collection of popular and new Songs, Marches, Waltzes, Dances, Rondos, Glees, Variations, Quadrilles, etc., both European and American publications. He will continue to manufacture and keep constantly on hand a large and fashionable assortment of Umbrellas and Parasols, at 28 Market street.[3]

The year 1839 may prove to be the initial date for the publication of sheet music in the Middle West, and Nathaniel Phillips will then be regarded as its first publisher.[4] In that year he

---

1. This would probably be the museum owned by Albert C. Koch. It consisted of three larger rooms, one filled with stuffed animals, the second with a large collection of wax figures of celebrities, and the third with a miscellaneous collection of odds and ends. In October of 1838, Koch turned paleontologist and began digging up the mastodon fossil skeletons that made him famous. The bones and skeletons were eventually exhibited in his museum. See J. F. McDermott, "Dr. Koch's Wonderful Fossils," *Bulletin of the Missouri Historical Society* 4 (July 1948): 233-56; also H. F. Osborne, *Proboscidia*, 2 vols. (New York, 1936-42), 1:90 and 783, 2:1374 and 1389.

2. File in the Missouri Historical Society (hereafter abbreviated MHS).

3. Reproduced in the rotogravure section of one of the local papers.

4. See Krohn, *Music Publishing in the Middle Western States before the Civil War*, Detroit Studies in Music Bibliography, 23 (Detroit: Information Coordinators, 1972), 13-14.

Fig. 4. G. H. Draper, St. Louis Grand March (St. Louis: N. Phillips, 1839), title-page

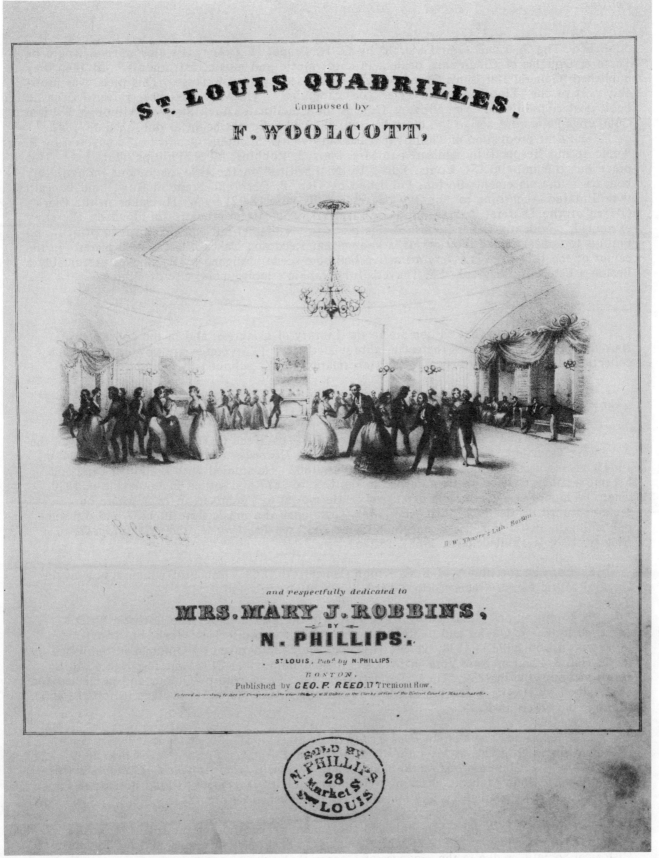

Fig. 5. F. Woolcott, St. Louis Quadrilles (St. Louis: N. Phillips, 184-?), title-page

published "The St. Louis Grand March" by G. H. Draper (Fig. 4).[5] His closest rival would be Tosso & Douglas of Cincinnati, dealers in sheet music and music instruments.[6] In 1840 they published "General Harrison's Grand March," composed by Joseph Tosso. This piece was probably part of the "Tippecanoe and Tyler Too" campaign.[7] The very next year Edward Lucas, a book dealer, published "The Citizens Guards' of Cincinnati Quick Step."[8] Although William Cummings Peters did not go to Louisville until 1829,[9] he did not begin to publish until 1842.[10]

The next production of Phillips that has survived is "St. Louis Quadrilles," composed by F. Woolcott and "respectfully dedicated to Mrs. Mary J. Robbins, by N. Phillips" (Fig. 5).[11] This piece has the imprint "St. Louis, Pub'd by N. Phillips" on the title-page, but immediately beneath it the statement "Boston, Published by Geo. P. Reed, 17 Tremont Row," and beneath that "Entered According to Act Of Congress in the year 184[?] by W. H. Oakes in the Clerk's Office of the District Court of Massachusetts." The last number is smudged on the copy examined. Evidently Oakes published this piece for Nathaniel but allowed Reed to print it and Phillips to appear in the imprint. It is known that Reed and Oakes interchanged plates. In the center of the title-page is a very attractive ballroom scene, designed by R. Cooke, presumably a Boston artist, and lithographed at Thayer's lithographic establishment, also of Boston.

------

5. Copies of the first edition are in the Library of Congress, and in the collection of Harold Linebeck of St. Louis (hereafter abbreviated HL). [Two copies are now in the Krohn collection at the Gaylord Music Library (information kindly supplied by George R. Keck).]

6. Data supplied by Martin F. Schmidt of the Louisville Public Library. See also *Appleton's Cyclopedia of American Biography*, 7 vols. (New York, 1888), 4:744, for Peters.

7. Copy in the Cincinnati Public Library. For Tosso, see O. D. Smith, "Joseph Tosso, the Arkansaw Traveller" in *Ohio State Archaeological and Historical Quarterly* 56 (January 1947): 16-45. Tosso was born in Mexico City, 3 August 1802. He studied with Baillot in Paris and became a concert violinist. He returned to the U.S. in 1817 and settled in Louisville in 1820, where he taught and concertized extensively. He moved to Cincinnati in 1827 where he remained until his death on 6 January 1887. Tosso opened a music store in 1837 and did some publishing in 1840. For "Tippecanoe and Tyler Too," see *The United States Encyclopedia of History*, 16 vols. (Philadelphia, 1968), 15:2752.

8. Copy in the library of E. C. Krohn (henceforth, ECK) [much of which is now at the Gaylord Music Library (henceforth, GML), Washington University].

9. Compositions published by W. C. Peters in the East include "The Danville Waltz," engraved by G. W. Quidor and published by Hewitt & Jacques in New York, but copyrighted by Peters in Louisville in 1838; "Peter's Highland March," engraved by Quidor and published by Firth, Hall & Pond of New York in 1845-47, their plate number 2172, but copyrighted by Peters at Louisville in 1839; "The Cincinnati Hop Waltz," engraved by Quidor and published and copyrighted by Hewitt & Jacques in 1839. "Peter's Highland March" is in the Cincinnati Public Library; the others in ECK.

10. W. Sutton, *The Western Book Trade* (Columbus, 1961), 82, states that Peters came to Cincinnati in 1839, giving as his authority J. T. Howard, *Stephen Foster* (New York, 1939), 124, who obviously got his information without acknowledgement from *Appleton's Cyclopedia* (see note 6 above). John Mullane, checking the Cincinnati City Directories, found no entries for Peters before 1846, neither has any music survived published before 1845.

11. Copy in ECK [at GML—this and subsequent verification of the specific location of parts of Krohn's collection, some of which he gave to St. Louis University and the Missouri Historical Society, is due to the kindness of George R. Keck].

The next piece available is definitely copyrighted in 1847 by Nathaniel Phillips, located at 42 Market Street. It bears the title "Vive la Dance," and is actually a pair of short waltzes "Composed and Respectfully Dedicated to the Ladies of St. Louis by Leopold de Meyer."[12] Famed as the "Lion of the Piano" and a redoubtable piano-pounder and exhibitionist, De Meyer had given three concerts here May 27, 29, and June 1 of 1846, and no doubt wished to show his appreciation of the enthusiastic reception given him.[13]

The performances of the Sable Harmonists, a group of blackface minstrels in St. Louis beginning the night of 17 November 1846, were probably responsible for the next of Nathaniel's publications. Nelson Kneass,[14] a member of the group, had made an arrangement of the minstrel song "Mary Blane."[15] A newspaper clipping attached to the copy in the Library of Congress reads: "A CARD: To the Public: the Sable Harmonists having sold their right and title in Number One of their *Melodies*, just published, to Mr. N. Phillips, No. 42 Market street, would respectfully state that copies of the song can only be obtained at his store." This song was copyrighted in 1847 and published with an elaborately designed title-page put on stone by E. Robyn and printed at the lithographic establishment of J. Hutawa (Fig. 6).[16] At each side are the medallions of the Sable Harmonists, Kneass, Huntley, and Roark to the left, and Plumer, Murphy, and Farrell to the right. At the top are two furled American flags surmounted by a spread eagle. At the bottom are grouped the instruments of the minstrels, a violin, tambourine, guitar, banjo, accordion, triangle, and "bones." In the center, the title "Songs of the Sable Harmonists, *Mary Blane*, words by Frederic Hunt, harmonized and arranged for the Piano Forte, by Nelson Kneass." The autograph signature of Fred Hunt found room in the left-hand corner. This was the most elaborate title-page that Nathaniel ever put forth, and it was produced in St. Louis.

What may prove to be the first original song published in St. Louis is the sentimental ballad entitled "The Hope Too Bright to Last, Composed and respectfully dedicated to Mrs. Taylor (of Cincinnati) by Charles Warren," copyrighted in 1847 by N. Phillips at 42 Market Street.[17] It covers three pages of music. The title-page is very ornate but has no specific illustration. The poetry of the song may be of interest:

> I dreamt a bright and glitt'ring star
> In lively radiance shone,
> And fondly deem'd its gentle rays
> Beam'd out for me alone.
>
> I lov'd it but too soon I saw
> The sky with clouds o'er cast,
> And found in sorrow I had dream'd
> Of hopes too bright to last.

---

12. Copy in ECK [at GML].

13. Program in MHS. See also H. C. Schonberg, *The Great Pianists* (New York, 1963), 179.

14. See Krohn, "Nelson Kneass: Minstrel Singer and Composer," *Yearbook: Inter-American Musical Research* 7 (1971): 17-41.

15. Copy in ECK [at GML], MHS, and the Library of Congress. [A facsimile of the title-page is also in Krohn, "Nelson Kneass," 33. —Ed.]

16. Julius Hutawa was at 7 North Second Street in 1842. In 1847-50 he was at 45 North Second. (He was sometimes associated with his brother Edward.)

17. Copy in ECK [at GML].

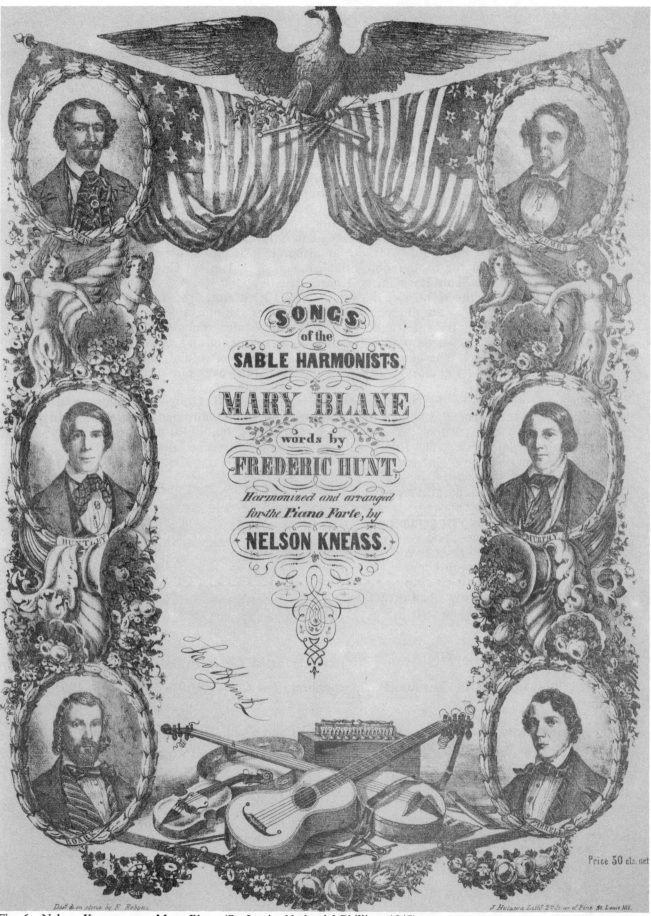

Fig. 6. Nelson Kneass, arr., Mary Blane (St. Louis: Nathaniel Phillips, 1847)

MARY BLANE

AS SUNG BY THE

SABLE HARMONISTS.

WORDS WRITTEN
BY
FRED HUNT
HARMONISED AND ARRANGED FOR THE
PIANO FORTE
BY
NELSON KNEASS

W.G. PLUMER

E.C. HUNTLEY

J. FARRELL

W. ROARK

J. MURPHY

N. KNEASS

St. Louis, Mo.
Published by

Nath¹ Phillips.
42 Market St.

Allegro

Moderato

coming back again, den farewell, den farewell, den farewell Mary Blane, oh do take care your

coming back

coming back

coming back

self my dear. I'm coming back again.

self my dear

self my dear

self my dear

2 When fust I saw her lubly Face
My fections she did gain.
And oft I hasten to de place
Where dwell't my Mary Blane.
Farewell &c.

3 We liv'd together many years
And she was still the same.
In joy and sorrow smiles and tears
I lov'd my Mary Blane.
Farewell &c.

4 Unto de Woods I went one day
A hunting ob de game.
De Indians came unto my hut
And stole my Mary Blane.
Farewell &c.

5 De time rolled on it greived me much
For me no tidings came.
I hunt dem woods both night and day
Till I found my Mary Blane.
Farewell &c.

6 I took her home unto my hut
My heart was in great pain.
But afore de sun did shine next day
Gone dead was Mary Blane.
Farewell &c.

I dreamed a rose in beauty bloomed
To all admirers free,
But that its soft and balmy breath
Was only shed for me.

I loved it but too soon there came
A rude and shiv'ring blast,
And taught me that I had dreamed again
Of hopes too bright to last.

In 1849, Nathaniel copyrighted "St. Louis Quickstep, in which are introduced the favorite airs of Oh! Susanna and Rosa Lee arranged for the Piano Forte."[18] This piece has no title-page; the outer pages are blank. Since Foster's "Oh! Susanna" had only been published in 1848, a pirated edition in New York February 25, and the authentic version in Louisville December 30, this was actually a quick pick-up. To be sure, the actual music bears little resemblance to either "Susanna" or "Rosa Lee."[19]

The Missouri Republican[20] issue of 8 May 1849 announced "This day was published *The Flirtation Waltz* composed by M. Strakosch and dedicated to Madame Casini. This waltz is considered one of the best of Strakosch's compositions and has only to be heard to be admired by everyone. Published and for sale at the counter of Nath'l Phillips', 42 Main street." The address should be Market and not Main Street. Maurice Strakosch was a Moravian pianist and impresario, the brother-in-law of Adelina Patti and the manager of her concerts. No copy of this waltz seems to have survived.[21]

An uncopyrighted "Les Bords du Rhin, Grand Valse Brillante composée par François Hunten" was issued about this time at 42 Market Street.[22] Franz Hünten was a prolific German composer who flourished at the time.[23] The surviving copy of this piece has no title-page. The music is printed on the inner seven pages, the last being blank. This piece was probably printed to supply the teaching demand. Another uncopyrighted piece was "Jenny Lind's Favorite Polka, Composed for the Piano Forte by A. Wallerstein"[24] and issued at 42 Market Street. Nathaniel must have felt the need of some kind of plate numbering, for the plates of this piece are stamped "B." This truly favorite polka must have been very popular, for it was reprinted by a half-dozen American publishers before Jenny Lind ever reached our shores. She landed in

---

18. Copy in HL [and GML].

19. See J. J. Fuld, *A Pictorial Bibliography of the First Editions of Stephen Foster* (Philadelphia, 1957), 18; also W. R. Whittlesey and O. G. Sonneck, *Catalogue of the First Editions of Stephen Foster* (Washington, 1915; reprint, New York: Da Capo, 1971), 52.

20. File in MHS.

21. See *Baker's Biographical Dictionary of Musicians*, 5th ed., ed. N. Slonimsky (New York, 1958), 1580.

22. Copy in ECK [at GML].

23. See *Baker's*, 751.

24. Copy in HL.

New York City on 1 September 1850.[25] Her concerts in St. Louis were given on March 18, 20, 22, 24, and 26 of 1851.[26]

The dramatic event of this early period was the Great Fire on the night of 17 May 1849.[27] This disaster devastated the whole riverfront, from Locust to Elm and back to Second Street. During the fire, the authorities decided to blow up a row of buildings in the path of the flames, hoping to save the Old Cathedral. Captain Targee of Missouri Fire Company Five successfully bombed five stores on the north side of Market Street. As he entered the sixth store, the bomb exploded prematurely and he was killed. One account states that the store to be blown up was McNeil's Hat Store, but while Captain Targee was on his way to the building, he said he was going to "blow up Phillips' store."[28] That could have been the store of James & J. R. Phillips which was presumably on the north side of Market Street at number 39.[29] Nathaniel's store was also burned out, and as he had taken out insurance in February, he had to sue the Protection Insurance Company for his insurance.[30] The court record gives quite an exciting picture of Nathaniel and his friends removing as much as possible of his stock. The music and musical instruments were temporarily stored in a room which he rented on Fourth Street. He subsequently occupied a store on Fourth Street before moving back to Market Street.

The first piece of music published after the fire seems to have been "Bellefontaine Waltz" by Charles Goetz, "Arranged for the Piano Forte and dedicated to Miss M. E. Waddington."[31] The copyright date is 1850 and the plate number is "C." There is no title-page, and no composer is mentioned. Bellefontaine was the name of a community in North St. Louis. Bearing the plate number "D," but having no copyright date, the next piece issued would be "Monticello Polka, Arranged for the Piano Forte by Henri Cramer."[32] This could be the H. Cramer listed in the City Directory for 1838-39 as "Professor of Music" and referred to casually by William Robyn in his autobiography: "I found one piano teacher who could not make his board and left. His name was Professor Cramer."[33] Where did Professor Cramer go? The Monticello in the title may refer to the community in Illinois or it could by some stretch of the imagination refer to the home of Thomas Jefferson. This is the first piece to bear the new address, which is

25. See E. Wagenknecht, *Jenny Lind* (Boston, 1931; reprint, New York: Da Capo, 1980), 5.

26. Programs in MHS. See also T. Papin, "Jenny Lind in St. Louis," *Music* 19 (November 1900): 20-34; also "Jenny Lind" in *Glimpses of the Past* 4 (April-June 1937): 47-50.

27. See T. E. Spencer, *The Story of Old St. Louis* (St. Louis, 1914), 158; also E. Kirschten, *Catfish and Crystal* (New York, 1960), 156-57.

28. See E. Edwards, *History of the Volunteer Fire Department of St. Louis* (St. Louis, 1906), 63-64.

29. No one seems to know on which side of the street the even or uneven numbers ran. 39 Market Street should have been on the north side of Market Street, yet later we find 131 Market Street opposite the Court House.

30. Missouri Supreme Court Reports, Jefferson City, 1852, pp. 220ff., Phillips vs. Protection Insurance Company.

31. Copy in ECK [at GML].

32. Copy in HL.

33. Krohn, ed., "The Autobiography of William Robyn," *Bulletin of the Missouri Historical Society* 9 (April 1953): 232-33. (Reprinted in *Missouri Music*, 154-55.)

given as 131 Market Street, Wymans Building. Still another polka, "The Cornelia Polka, Composed for the Piano Forte by H. Walther," was dedicated to Miss S. Stickney.[34] The copyright claim is for 1850, but there is no plate number.

A more ambitious piece is "Les Adieux," a "Nocturne pour le Piano Forte composé by B. A. Bode" and dedicated to Madame K. Fuller.[35] The imprint on the title-page gives no address but the copyright claim is dated 1850. The music fills four plates, and the title-page is ornate without being pictorial. Bernard August Bode was an outstanding piano teacher and theoretician.[36] His most noted pupil was the composer Hermann Strachauer.[37] Bode performed the "Fantasie e variationi de bravoura" composed by Theodore Döhler on themes from Donizetti's *Anna Bolena* at the concert on the Philharmonic Society, 6 March 1862.[38]

Now we have a brace of songs to consider. "I Love the Merry Sunshine," a "Ballad written by J. W. Lake, Esq., Music composed by Stephen Glover,"[39] was a popular English song, reprinted by eight other American publishers from the original English edition. The music spreads over three pages, and the song bears an engraved title-page. Another British favorite was the ballad "I Am Dreaming of Thee,"[40] composed by the prolific English song writer George Alexander Lee and reprinted by seven other American publishers. The title-page announced that this "Napolitaine" was "sung with great applause by Madame Biscaccianti."[41] Signora Eliza Ostinelli Biscaccianti, the American prima donna,[42] had given the concerts here, March 20 and 22 of 1850, and the song was probably reprinted to meet popular demand.[43]

A song about which we know little is "The Worth of Time" by James Schobe, copyrighted in 1850.[44] It is listed in the *Board of Music Trade Catalogue* of 1870,[45] but no copy seems to have survived. "The Egyptian Girl's Song," with "Poetry by Mrs. J. S. Howe and the Music composed and respectfully dedicated to Miss S. Pomeroy by E. C. Davis"[46] was copyrighted by Nathaniel Phillips in 1850 and has a very ornate title-page designed by "Campbell, Sc." The "Campbell" may have been the Robert L. Campbell of 25 Chestnut Street and listed in the City

---

34. Copy in HL.

35. Copy at GML.

36. See Krohn, *Century*, 103.

37. Krohn, *Century*, 130.

38. Program in MHS.

39. Copy at GML.

40. Copy in ECK [at GML].

41. See J. D. Brown and S. S. Stratton, *British Music Biography* (Birmingham, 1897), 242.

42. See J. W. Moore, *Complete Encyclopedia of Music* (Boston, 1854), 144; also G. E. Schiavo, *Italian-American History*, 2 vols. (New York, 1947), 1:254-56.

43. Programs in MHS.

44. See Krohn, *Century*, 12.

45. *Board of Music Trade Catalogue* (1870; reprint, New York: Da Capo, 1973).

46. Copy in HL [and the title-page only at GML, according to George Keck].

Directory as an engraver.[47] The composer, Edward Cox Davis, was a native of Baltimore who at the end of the Civil War resided in Des Moines, Iowa. He is chiefly notable for his "Lincoln's Funeral March," published by Balmer & Weber in 1865,[48] but was originally conceived in 1861 as a funeral march for General Nathaniel Lyon, who was killed at Wilson's Creek in southwest Missouri, 10 August 1861.[49]

And now Nathaniel became more conscious of plate numbers. The next piece to have survived is still an 1850 copyright. "La Polka, as danced by Mon'r Henri and Mad'me Javelli, arranged for the Piano Forte by Nelson Kneass" is still in the old format.[50] For the first time the heading states that 131 Market Street is "opposite the Court House." The plate number at the bottom of the page is 21. Did Nathaniel enumerate his entire production up to this point and then actually number this composition? Or are twenty pieces missing since the last song discussed? We will never know until the missing numbered pieces turn up.

To get back to "La Polka," Nelson Kneass, who is credited with the arrangement of the same, is the musician who arranged the "Mary Blane" that Nathaniel published in 1847.[51] He is known as the composer of the musical setting of the poem "Ben Bolt" by Thomas Dunn English, which was published in 1848 by W. C. Peters & Company of Louisville and by 1850 was basking in the glare of a terrific popularity. In 1846, Kneass became a member of the Sable Harmonists, and it was while he was with this group of wandering minstrels that he composed "Ben Bolt" and many other fine songs. He died in Chillicothe, Missouri on 10 September 1868.

Whatever piece bore the plate number 22 has not survived. The next number, 23, was assigned to the "California Quiver Polka, composed and affectionately dedicated to her pupils by Mrs. E. Sanderson,"[52] obviously a contemporary piano teacher. This piano piece was copyrighted in 1850. Why it was named "California Quiver" we will never know, but since the whole country was in a mad rush to California in search of gold any reference to that state would be significant. The next two plate numbers are missing, so that we now have to deal with 26, "Rosebloom Polka."[53] The composer, John Wogtech, was but following the current trend in dance composition. His piano piece was copyrighted in 1850 and recopyrighted in 1852. It was then sold to Balmer & Weber and acquired their plate number 410=2. The reprint of a popular piece by Franz Hünten, "Gallopade Quadrille," bore the Phillips plate number 27.[54] Charles Goetz composed the "Jefferson Barracks Waltz" which he published in 1851 and dedicated to Sallie Walker with the plate number 28.[55] This may be the last piece that Nathaniel published, for he seems to have sold his entire catalog to Balmer & Weber in 1852. He continued in business as dealer in pianos, his last directory entry being in 1859 at Fifth and Locust. After that he left St. Louis and returned to Boston, his birthplace.

---

47. In 1851 he was at 36 North Second.

48. Copy in ECK. [Plate no. 1482-3. —Information supplied by Richard D. Wetzel. George Keck reports that three copies are at GML.]

49. See DAB 11:534.

50. Copy in HL.

51. For Kneass, see note 14, above.

52. Copy in HL.

53. Copy in HL.

54. Copy in HL.

55. Copy in HL.

Phillips

The charmingly written memorial that his son Samuel R. Phillips presented to the Missouri Historical Society, presumably in 1911, may serve to characterize Nathaniel Phillips, the man. It is engrossed on a large sheet of parchment and has a beautifully illuminated border of flowers on the left side framing a fine photograph of Nathaniel.[56] The text follows:[57]

> Nathaniel Phillips, one of the early St. Louis merchants, was born at Boston in 1811. He was a lineal descendant of Ann Hutchinson, who caused the great dissensions soon after the settlement of Boston, and who was driven into exile and murdered by Indians near New York. Mr. Phillips came to St. Louis in 1835 and opened his store on Market street, dealing in music, pianos, and military goods. The store was beautifully fitted up, and in its day was one of the show places of the city. It was destroyed in the fire of 1849. Mr. Phillips published the first sheet music west of the Ohio river. Hiram Powers'[58] celebrated statue of the *Greek Slave* was shown in the store above mentioned.[59]

56. Preserved in MHS, Division of Pictures.

57. DAB 9:436-37.

58. DAB 15:158-60; also *American Heritage History of American Antiques* (New York, 1968), 162-63.

59. Samuel's memory probably played him false, for he missed his father's retirement and return to Boston by several years. The Registry Division of the City of Boston, consulting the birth indices from 1800 to 1848, could find no record of the birth of Nathaniel. It did certify his death as of 27 March 1892 at age eighty years and eleven months, which would place his birth in April of 1811. Both his father, also Nathaniel, and his mother, whose maiden name was Margaret Buckman, were natives of Boston. In October of 1904, Samuel wrote to Mary Louise Dalton, librarian of the Missouri Historical Society, expressing his surprise that a portrait of Governor Thomas Reynolds was not on exhibition in the Society's galleries. He subsequently bequeathed to the Society a portrait of his mother, but it was not accepted. (The letters are on file in the archives of the MHS.)

4

THE UNRELATED PHILLIPS

The City Directory of 1845 that contains the full-page advertisement of Nathaniel Phillips also contains on the page opposite a similar announcement of James Phillips.[1] The text on page 196 is headed "NEW MUSIC STORE." There follows a drawing of an assorted group of music instruments, topped by three opened umbrellas and a stand of walking canes. The text runs on: "Umbrella, Parasol, and Cane Manufactory (Sign of the Golden Violin), No. 40, North Second between Pine and Chestnut Streets, St. Louis, Mo." A detailed description of the stock of musical instruments and musical merchandise ensues. Toward the bottom of the page we are told in bold type "Instruction Books and Music for all instruments in great variety, also Backgammon Men and Boards, Dominoes, Dice and Chessmen. Umbrellas and Parasols covered and repaired." There is a final *nota bene*: "The above establishment is not connected with any other music store in this city." The whole advertisement is signed "James Phillips, Agent." Friendly relations between the brothers, if they were related, were not excessive. In the City Directory of 1847, we have a similar full-page advertisement, but this time James announces his location as Apollo Hall, 39 Market Street, and the firm name is given as J. & J. R. Phillips.[2] The new store was presumably right across the street from that of Nathaniel.

The first intimation we have that James & J. R. Phillips are interested in publishing is to be found in the heading of the "simon pure" "Nightingale Waltz" published and copyrighted by Oliver Ditson of Boston in 1846, with J. & J. R. Phillips in the heading as secondary publishers.[3] There is no title-page, and the music is printed on the inner two pages with the Ditson plate number 1229. This piece turned up in the *Board of Music Trade Catalogue* of 1870, so it was obviously a good seller.

The appearance of the Sable Harmonists on the local scene was undoubtedly responsible for the next "J. & J. R." effusion. The composition in question is "Lou'siana Belle, composed and arranged for the piano-forte," with the copyright dated 1847.[4] This was nothing less than a steal from the "Lou'siana Belle, written for and sung by Joseph Murphy of the Sable Harmonists," published and copyrighted by W. C. Peters of Cincinnati in 1847. No composer is mentioned, but according to Morrison Foster it was Stephen's first black minstrel song--and in fact his third publication, the first being "Open Thy Lattice Love" published in 1844.[5] Since the Peters edition of "Lou'siana Belle" was not entered for copyright until 18 October 1846, the Phillips version was jotted down from memory by one of the Sable Harmonists, either Joseph Donnelly Murphy or Nelson Kneass.

---

1. See *Green's St. Louis Directory (No. 1) for 1845* (St. Louis: James Green, 1844).

2. See *St. Louis Business Directory for 1847* (St. Louis, 1847).

3. Copy in ECK [two at GML, according to George Keck].

4. Copy in MHS.

5. Facsimile available in *Foster Hall Reproductions of Songs, Compositions, and Arrangements by Stephen C. Foster* (Indianapolis: privately printed by Josiah Kirby Lilly, 1933).

The music is printed on the two inner pages. The title-page is a lithograph of an attractive girl with long curls and a natty bonnet. The melody of the song is practically identical in both versions, but the piano accompaniment is more elaborate in the Phillips edition and the rhythm is more complicated. The words are also slightly different. In the Peters version the first verse runs

> Oh! Louisiana's the same old state
> Whar' Massa us'd to dwell,
> He had a lubly cullud gal,
> 'Twas the Lou'siana Belle.

In the Phillips publication the first verse states that

> Lou'siana is dat good old state,
> Where Massa used to dwell,
> He used to own a pretty yellow gal,
> She was the Lou'siana Belle.

There are five verses in the Phillips opus, while the original has only four. The Phillips piece was probably deposited for copyright to warrant the claim of 1847 as the year of copyright protection. This type of pirating of Foster songs was rather commonplace.[6] The authorized editions of "Uncle Ned" and of "Susanna" were deposited by W. C. Peters of Louisville on 30 December 1848.[7]

The first pirated edition of "Oh! Susanna" was deposited by C. Holt of New York City, 25 February 1848, and of "Old Uncle Ned" by William C. Millet of New York City that May 16.[8] This type of unethical procedure was due to Foster's practice of handing out manuscript copies of his songs to different minstrel singers in the hope that they would use them in their shows. At the outset, he was not sure of the selling qualities of his songs; in fact, he did not have any idea that they might be commercially valuable. He gave the manuscripts of "Lou'siana Belle" and "Old Uncle Ned" to William Cummings Peters of Louisville. When "Uncle Ned" began selling like hotcakes, he was brought to a realization of the commercial value of his compositions, and decided to devote himself to composition as an occupation instead of a hobby.[9]

The Sable Harmonists were also responsible for the "J. & J. R." publications. The ditty "Mary Blane" was another song in the black minstrel style of which "Lou'siana Belle" was a part. Nathaniel issued the Kneass arrangement (see Fig. 6 above, pp. 20-23) about the same time that "J. & J. R." put forth two more versions.[10] These songs were very crudely engraved on two plates each. One bears a title-page with the Sable Harmonists stretched in a row across the page. They are playing their instruments which consisted of a violin, a guitar, a banjo, an

---

6. M. Foster, *My Brother Stephen* (Indianapolis, 1932), 34.

7. See W. R. Whittlesey and O. G. Sonneck, *Catalogue of First Editions of Stephen C. Foster* (Washington, 1915; reprint, New York: Da Capo, 1971), 42 and 52.

8. See J. J. Fuld, *A Pictorial Bibliography of the First Editions of Stephen C. Foster* (Philadelphia, 1957), 18-19.

9. See J. T. Howard, *Stephen Foster* (New York, 1939), 134-46; H. V. Milligan, *Stephen Foster* (New York, 1920), 44-47; E. F. Morneweck, *Chronicles of Stephen Foster's Family*, 2 vols. (Pittsburgh, 1944), 1:307-15.

10. Copy in HL [at GML].

accordion, a tambourine, and castanets or "bones" as they were usually designated.[11] This was the one combination of blackface comedians that enjoyed such a vogue throughout the United States about this time.

In the other edition, the title-page was graced with the same comely wench who had served as adornment of "Lou'siana Belle." "Mary Blane" originated in England, for the words were written by the popular Irish poet Wellington Guernsey, and the music was composed by the prolific song writer George Arthur Barker.[12] Fortunately, the British Library has preserved a copy of the original edition of this minstrel classic which was published in London by J. Williams of 123 Cheapside and entered at Stationer's Hall 28 July 1846.[13] The song may have been written upon the occasion of the visit of the Ethiopian Serenaders, an American minstrel troupe, to London in that year. Possibly at the same time Guernsey also wrote "You'll See Dem on de Ohio," which according to its title-page was also "sung by the Ethiopian Serenaders at St. James' Theatre" and was published by the same Williams. It is this title-page that announces Guernsey as the "author of Mary Blane." So far as the melody is concerned, the Kneass and the "J. & J. R. II" are identical except that the Kneass is in A major and the other in F. "J. & J. R. I" has four measures that are completely different. Somebody's memory failed to recall the orthodox line. The words of the first verse of the two "J. & J. R." texts differ too. One version tells us

> I fell in lob wid a yellow gal,
> I'll tell you what's her name;
> She libs in old Missouri,
> And her name is Mary Blane.

And the other that

> I once did love a yellow gal,
> I'll tell you what's her name,
> She came from Old Virginia,
> And they call her Mary Blane.

The third verse which is the same in both J. & J. R. issues, and is lacking in the Kneass, has it that

> St. Louis boasts of pretty gals,
> But Oh! 'tis all in vain,
> They have no gal that fills my eye,
> As does my Mary Blane.

The Kneass "yellow gal" also "came from old Virginia," but the second line reads "I'll tell you all her name." The two "J. & J. R." texts have seven verses, identical except that the fourth verse

---

11. For other illustrations, see H. Nathan, *Dan Emmett and the Rise of Early Negro Minstrelsy* (Norman, 1962), 124, 141, 148, 149, 152; and E. L. Rice, *Monarchs of Minstrelsy* (New York, 1911), 21, 45, 69, 93, 117, 141.

12. Xerox copy in ECK. See also J. D. Brown and S. S. Stratton, *British Musical Biography* (Birmingham, 1897), 26, 176. In a search for additional data on these songs, recourse was had to D. Ewen's *American Popular Songs* (New York, 1966). His unreliability was soon apparent. The entry on "Mary Blane" is completely incorrect. "Open Thy Lattice Love" and Lou'siana Belle" are both declared to be Foster's first publications, and "Uncle Ned" the second.

13. Copy in ECK. See also C. Humphries and W. C. Smith, *Music Publishing in the British Isles* (London, 1954), 335.

of the "J. & J. R. II" is the same as the third verse of Kneass. The latter has only six verses of which the second, fourth, fifth, and sixth are entirely different than their "J. & J. R." counterparts.

We have in "Mary Blane" mention of the same "yaller gal" that we heard about in "Lou'siana Belle," "Yaller Gal," "My Pretty Yaller Gal," and many others. These songs are all part of a "yaller gal" tradition, a "yaller gal" being an attractive female mulatto. Minstrel songs do not all maintain the plantation dialect but frequently lapse into a more northern, even English, idiom.[14] In true folksong style, the words and frequently the music vary from one version to the other. A collection that may claim to represent the contemporary versions of the songs discussed so far is *The Ethiopian Glee Book*, "containing the songs sung by the Christy Minstrels with many other popular Negro Melodies," compiled by Gumbo Chaff, A.M.A., "First Banjo Player to the King of Congo" and published at Boston by Elias Howe in 1849.[15]

An "Apollo Hall" series was started by "J. & J. R." sometime in the 1840s. The earliest piece, number 3, is an "Opera Mazurka" which is printed as usual on the inner two pages but is devoid of a composer or a copyright claim.[16] Then we have the song "Bonny Mary, Words by a Friend, the Music composed and respectfully dedicated to Miss Mary E. Barrett of St. Louis, Mo., by Wm. Robyn."[17] This was no. 5 of the Apollo Hall series, published and sold by "J. & J. R. Phillips, Apollo Hall, 39 Market street." The copyright claim at the bottom of the page is dated 1846. The foregoing fills two-thirds of what could be called the title-page. Beneath the heading are the first two systems of music. The rest of the music occupies the inner two pages.

Since J. & J. R. Phillips did not use plate numbers, there is no way of determining the sequence of their remaining issues. The "Rossignol Polka" exists in two editions. What may be the first edition consists of the inner two pages of music. The heading over the left page reads "Rossignol Polka as danced by Monsieur Henry and Madame L. Javelli and Mons. G. de Korponay, St. Louis, Published by J. & J. N. Phillips, Apollo Hall."[18] The copy available carries the Balmer & Weber plate number 1393 at the bottom of both pages.[19] The J. N. is obviously an error for J. R. What may be the second edition is graced by the addition of a dancing couple. Beneath the dancers stands the title as before, but minus the "Mons. G. de Korponay."[20] The heading over the music is the same as in the first edition, but minus the publisher's name. The music plates have been re-engraved.

A much more attractively drawn dancing couple ornaments the title-page of "Aurelia Polka, Composed and respectfully dedicated to Geo. I. Murray E^{sq}. by A. Waldauer, Leader of the St. Louis Theatre," copyrighted by J. & J. R. Phillips in 1847 (Fig. 7).[21] August Waldauer fluctuated between New Orleans and St. Louis from 1844 to 1851. He became leader of the St. Louis Varieties Theatre in 1852, and eventually became conductor of the St. Louis Philharmonic

---

14. See S. Spaeth, *Weep Some More My Lady* (New York, 1927), 103-17; Nathan, *Dan Emmett*, 159-213; *Glimpses of the Past*, November 1935, 142-45.

15. See *Ethiopian Glee Book*, 156, 99 [the copy at the Library of Congress is dated 1848; information supplied by James R. Heintze].

16. Copy in ECK [at GML].

17. Copy in ECK.

18. Copy in the Library of Congress.

19. Copy in ECK [at GML].

20. Copy in ECK [two copies at GML].

21. Copies in ECK [at GML] and HL.

Fig. 7. A. Waldauer, Aurelia Polka (St. Louis: J. & J. R. Phillips, 1847), title-page

Orchestra during the season 1866-67 and of the Musical Union Orchestra from 1881 to 1890.[22] He was a prolific composer.

The same dancing couple used on the title-page of "Aurelia Polka" also figures on the title-page of "Apollo Waltz, Composed and respectfully dedicated to Edward C. Winchester, Esq., by W. Robyn."[23] The lithographed title-pages of both pieces were printed by J. H. Bufford Lithographic Establishment of Boston, and "Apollo Waltz" was also copyrighted in 1847. William Robyn came to St. Louis in 1837 and was Professor of Music at St. Louis University from 1838 to 1852.[24] He was a fine cellist and composed numerous piano pieces as well as an excellent piano trio.

The crowning achievement of the J. & J. R. catalog was "Col. Doniphan's Grand March, resp'ly dedicated to the Officers and Members of the Missouri Volunteers, by the Publishers. Composed by A. Waldouer [*sic* = Waldauer], Leader of the Orchestra of the St. Louis Theatre" (Fig. 8).[25] This piano piece was copyrighted and published in 1847 with a stunning title-page designed by Leon Pomarede, the St. Louis artist, and printed by Bufford & Company of Boston.[26] Colonel Doniphan on a spirited horse, with cavalrymen in the background, occupies the center of the title-page. Below are pictured the coat-of-arms of the State of Missouri and a group of furled flags. To each side stand spears bearing banners on which are inscribed the names of the conquered cities--Taos, Sacramento, Chihuahua, Santa Fe. It was in 1847 that Colonel Alexander William Doniphan led his First Regiment of Missouri Mounted Volunteers south in one of the most brilliant of long marches to capture the cities mentioned above.[27] His success made him a popular hero worthy of the music dedicated to him.

After the Great Fire, James Phillips carried on in Apollo Hall, now located at 44 Market Street. His one surviving publication bearing his own name, not J. & J. R. Phillips, is "Concert Hall Favorite Waltz, Composed by G. W. [*recte*: J. W.] Postlewaite, respectfully dedicated to Mr. Xaupi and his pupils by the publisher."[28] This piece was probably published for James by Oliver Ditson of Boston, for it bears his copyright claim of 1850 and his plate number 1845. Moreover, it appears in the *Board of Music Trade Catalogue* of 1870 as a Ditson publication. The composer, Joseph William Postlewaite, was a gifted black musician who also became a publisher.[29] Mr. Xaupi was a popular dancing instructor who conducted a flourishing school for

22. See Krohn, *A Century of Missouri Music* (St. Louis, 1924), 132.

23. Copy in HL.

24. See Krohn, *Century*, 125; also Krohn, ed., "The Autobiography of William Robyn," *Bulletin of the Missouri Historical Society* 9 (January-April 1953): 141-54, 230-55, reprinted in *Missouri Music*, 239-55.

25. Copies in ECK [at GML] and HL.

26. See J. F. McDermott, "Leon Pomarede, Our Parisian Knight of the Easel," *Bulletin of the City Art Museum* 34, no. 1 (winter 1949): 8-18.

27. See DAB 5:365; R. A. Billington, *Westward Expansion* (New York, 1949), 580; *American Heritage Pictorial Atlas of United States History* (New York, 1966), 162-63.

28. Copy in MHS.

29. See Krohn, *Century*, 123; also J. C. Cotter, "The Negro in Music in St. Louis" (A.M. thesis in Music Education, Washington University, 1959). [See also Samuel A. Floyd, Jr., "A Black Composer in Nineteenth-Century St. Louis," *19th Century Music* 4, no. 2 (fall 1980): 121-33. —Ed.]

Fig. 8. A. Waldouer [Waldauer], Col. Doniphan's Grand March (St. Louis: J. & J. R. Phillips, 1847), title-page

dancing. Concert Hall, located at 38-40 Market Street, was opened with a brilliant concert 30 December 1839,[30] and was a commodious auditorium, seating one thousand persons.

James & J. R. may not have published anything after 1850; at least nothing seems to have survived. James probably sold his catalog to Balmer & Weber at the same time Nathaniel sold out. Neither James nor J. R. are in the City Directory of 1852, 1852-53, 1853-54, or later. They may have left St. Louis.

_____

30. Program in MHS.

5

A MOTLEY CREW

As early as 1848, John Gass seems to have opened a music store at 38 North Second Street.[1] In 1849, he copyrighted the song "I Dreamt That You Loved Me" by Henry Robyn.[2] The next year he copyrighted the ballad "Queen of the West" by W. W. Rossington.[3] The words to both of them were written by Henry F. Watson. Now he seems to have acquired a partner, and as John Gass & Company began using plate numbers. Number 204-2 is the song "The Romaika,"[4] a poem in Thomas Moore's *Evenings in Greece*. The music was composed by Moore, but since there is no copyright claim it cannot be dated. Number 283-1 is the one-page print of the "Prussian March in Abelino."[5] Again, there is no copyright claim. "Abelino" is the play *Abaellino der grosse Bandit* by the German writer Heinrich Zschokke that had been translated by William Dunlap and first performed at New York, 11 February 1801.[6] Noah M. Ludlow produced this play at St. Louis during 1820.[7]

Wakelam & Iucho at 29 Fourth Street advertised themselves as sole agents for the Firth, Pond & Company's celebrated pianos in 1853, and incidentally mentioned the fact that they were music publishers. From 1857 to 1860, William Wakelam carried on alone. None of their publications seems to have survived.

Henry and William Robyn[8] launched a novel undertaking in 1851. They named their publication *Polyhymnia: A Musical Anthology for the Piano-Forte Published in Monthly Numbers* (Fig. 9), and projected a series of monthly numbers running from January through December. Only the issues for January, February, and March have survived. The number for January may serve as an example, for it contains a "Polonaise" and a "Charlotte Polka" by William Robyn, "Clara Polka," the "Orange Blossom Waltz," the "Evening Star Polka," the nocturne "Le Désir," and the song "The Dream of Home" by Henry Robyn, as well as a piano transcription of a duet from the opera *Beatrice di Tenda*, presumably by Bellini.[9]

---

1. Krohn, *Missouri Music*, 10.

2. Copy at GML; title-page + 3 plates.

3. Xerox copy; title-page + 3 plates.

4. Copy at GML; heading and 2 plates, no. 204-2.

5. Copy at GML, plate 283-1.

6. W. Kosch, *Deutsches Literature Lexikon* (Bern, 1963), 508.

7. N. Ludlow, *Dramatic Life as I Found It* (St. Louis, 1880; reprint, Blom, 1966), 192-93.

8. Krohn, *Missouri Music*, 125, 239-55.

9. Copy at GML; title-page + 12 plates.

Fig. 9. William and Henry Robyn, *Polyhymnia: A Musical Anthology for the Piano-Forte Published in Monthly Numbers* (St. Louis, 1851), title-page

Carl Fritz was at 52 Fourth Street when he copyrighted in 1857 "Amazon Polka" by C. M. Mueller, and in 1858 when he published "Josephine Mazurka" (plate 83-3) by Franz Staab.[10] Fritz & Derleth were at 42 Market Street when they published "The Gipsy Polka" (plate 42) by J. J. Strauss[11] and "Loreley" by Silcher. This may have been their location when they published "Honderü (Hungarian Quadrilles)" by Ladislaus Kovats.[12] None of these can be dated because they were not entered for copyright.

"St. Louis Volunteers Quickstep"[13] by Francis Woolcott was copyrighted by W. M. Harlow in 1861 in the District Court of Eastern Missouri, although it was actually printed for Harlow by the O. Ditson Company of Boston.[14] The songs "Thy Voices Still Are Dear to Me" by Mrs. E. C. Comstock[15] and "Is That Mother Bending o'er Me" by Charles H. Greene[16] were copyrighted and published by Harlow at St. Louis in 1863.

A unique item has survived from this approximate period. It consists of the orchestral parts of a "Collection of Dances, arranged for the orchestra by A. Held, Professor of Music."[17] The music is octavo in size and according to the imprint on the cover was published at Magdeburg in Prussia. The local publisher was Koenig, Trauernight & Company, located at 82 Franklin Avenue, in 1860. The partners included Lorenzo Koenig, Theodore Trauernight, and Charles Schwerdfeger.

The New York Music Store was opened at 36 Market Street by Henry Sherburne in 1853 and remained there until 1867. Two of his publications have survived, "Florilla Schottische," copyrighted in 1864, and "Arranita Polka," dated 1866, both composed by S. T. Bravoula.

J. Ballhouse, who in 1855 was located at 52 Fourth Street, functioned as the publisher of the songs "The Lost Flower" by George W. Beckel and "Bonnie Belle of Santa Fe" by J. C. Beckel,[18] both copyrighted by their respective composers in 1855.

------

10. Copy at GML; title-page + 3 plates, no. 83-3.

11. Xerox copy at GML; heading and 2 plates, no. 42. [I cannot verify this title nor which Strauss this is. —Ed.]

12. [Copy at GML.]

13. On the Volunteers, see the article on Nathaniel Lyon in DAB 11:534-35.

14. [Copy at GML.]

15. [Copy at GML, dated 1863; title-page + 3 plates.]

16. [Copy at GML, dated 1863; title-page + 3 plates.]

17. [Copy at GML.]

18. [Copy at GML.]

6

ON SOLID GROUND WITH BALMER & WEBER

Johann Heinrich Weber, *Geheimer Hofrath*, at Coblenz on the Rhine, married Ida Rosalie Banda, a lady of Jewish extraction. Such an alliance was frowned upon by the royal court at Coblenz, and Weber eventually found it advisable to leave Germany. He came to America in 1834 and settled in St. Charles on the Missouri River with his wife and family of five. His daughter Therese became a fine soprano and a talented pianist. His son Carl Heinrich became an excellent cellist, and another son, Carl Gottwalt, an expert double-bass player.

At about the same time, Gottfried Balmer left his comfortable home in Mühlhausen and came to the U.S. He went to Philadelphia and then to St. Louis sometime in 1836. His son Charles left the family at Philadelphia and went to New Orleans, hoping to see more of the country. Charles had been a child prodigy who before his tenth year had learned to play the piano, organ, violin, and clarinet. At sixteen he was assistant conductor of the orchestra at the Göttingen Conservatory of Music. While a student at the conservatory he made copies of many chamber music compositions that he possibly could not afford to buy.

Arrived in New Orleans, he met the concert singer Madame Caradori Allan, who engaged him as her accompanist. In the course of one of their tours they reached St. Louis and Balmer decided to make St. Louis his home. This was in 1839.

On 1 May 1840 Balmer married Therese Weber, and their home at 160 South Fourth Street became the center of musical life in St. Louis. Visiting artists were entertained there as a matter of course. Musicians of the stature of Henri Vieuxtemps, Ole Bull, and Louis Moreau Gottschalk became part of the family. In 1848, in partnership with his brother-in-law, Balmer opened a music store at 141 Market Street.

Balmer had begun to compose when he settled in St. Louis. He wrote many songs and piano pieces that were published by William Cummings Peters at Lexington, Kentucky. In 1842 he published his "Saint Louis Firemen's Parade March" at his own expense. A popular piece was his "Concert Hall Cotillion." This was copyrighted by Balmer & Weber in 1848 and the plate number was 31. Balmer's arrangement of "Natalie Waltz" by J. Labitzky, number 44, was published in 1850. There are several uncopyrighted compositions among which may be listed plate 46, "Yankee Doodle"; 53, "Louisville Grand March"; 61, "Aria alla Scozzese" with variations by Thomas Valentine; 62, "Bonaparte's Retreat from Moscow" arranged by J. Schell; 64, "Home as a Waltz" (a new arrangement of Henry R. Bishop's "Home Sweet Home"); 66, "The Land of Sweet Erin"; 71, "King of the Sea" by Edwin Ransford; 75, "Russian March"; and 77, "Bristol March" by Oliver Shaw. These were probably all published in 1850. This is also the year of Balmer's composition "The Star I Love," plate 160.[1]

It is rather odd to find Balmer's piece "St. Louis Serenading Waltz," an 1848 copyright, numbered 176. "Concert Hall Cotillion," originally numbered 31, is now reissued and renumbered 177.[2] Another peculiarity is the rise of double numbering, so that we have the vocal duet

---

1. [Copies of all cited in this paragraph, except Ransford's "King of the Sea" and Balmer's "The Star I Love," are at GML.]

2. [Copy at GML.]

"Bear Me Boatlet," "Gently Gliding" by Sigmund Neukomm, and "St. Louis Serenading Waltz,"[3] all numbered 176. Number 177 was shared by "Concert Hall Cotillion" and Balmer's "Pacific Railroad Grand March." The use of the same number for two compositions may have been due to carelessness. In fact, only one other instance has survived. "The Angels Whisper" by Samuel Lover and Charles Grobe's "Farewell if Ever Fondest Prayer" were numbered 171.[4] Another peculiarity is the use of the double hyphen in plate numbers, so that we have 18=4. This is done continuously and thus constitutes a Balmer & Weber trademark.

Most publishers did not copyright reprints. Since they were common property there was no point in paying for protection. The copyright fee could be saved. Practically all original compositions were given copyright protection. However, even that did not prevent irresponsible publishers from stealing whatever struck their fancy.

When Balmer & Weber announced in the *Anzeiger des Westens* issue of 3 June 1848 that they were going to open a music store, they neglected to give the address. The listing in the City Directory for 1848 located the store at 141 Market Street. In 1851 they moved to 58 North Fourth Street. A slight shift in 1857 took them to 56 North Fourth Street.

Ten years later they occupied 209 North Fourth Street, but only stayed there two years. 1869 found them at 206 North Fifth Street. By 1878 they held forth at 311 North Fifth Street, which became Broadway in 1884. They returned to 209 North Fourth Street in 1888, then in 1894 moved to Olive Street. They were at 908 from 1894 to 1902. The World's Fair year found them at 1109, and finally in 1907 they settled at 1004. This was their location when they closed up shop later that year. They sold their music catalog to Leo Feist of New York. He started to transport the entire stock to New York by ship. Unfortunately, the vessel foundered off the New Jersey coast, and the Balmer & Weber catalog found a watery grave. Meanwhile, Adam Shattinger bought the musical merchandise in the store and moved it to his own store at 910 Olive Street.

Balmer & Weber were successful from the start and soon absorbed their competitors. In 1852 they bought the catalogs of Nathaniel Phillips and J. & J. R. Phillips. In the course of time they acquired the music of Sherburne, Pilcher, Gass, and several others. They catered to the teacher, and published innumerable teaching pieces. With so much classic and romantic music available it would seem unnecessary to publish more. It must not be forgotten that the great composers did not have the ultimate consumer in view. Not being piano teachers, they were not aware of the problems confronting the practical piano teacher.

A piece would start with simplicity only to merge into a passage of the utmost difficulty. The conception of grades of difficulty did not occur to the great masters. In order to teach piano in an orderly manner, a teacher should have available a series of graduated texts. Editors and publishers have tried to isolate the different types of technical difficulty in groups, usually called grades. The number of grades may run from six to eleven, with seven as the common denominator. Nowhere was there a description of the specifications of any particular grade. Editors and publishers developed an unwritten code of grading that guided them for many years, in fact over fifty. It was not until the twentieth century that something more tangible developed.

Since publishers were in business to sell music, it was of the utmost importance that their so-called "teaching pieces" should sell. The problem was to contrive a piano piece that would fit into a given grade and at the same time possess charm. No formula has ever been discovered that would assure popularity. Fortunately, a tribe of minor composers appeared with the ability to write teaching pieces that would sell. To this category belong composers like Gustave Lange, Heinrich Englemann, Carl Wilhelm Kern, and Carl Bohm.

When Balmer & Weber started to publish, they were not committed to any definite method of procedure. Here are "Serenading Polka" of Charles Balmer and "Grand Hungarian March" of

---

3. [Copy at GML.]

4. [Copy at GML.]

Joseph Gungl, copyrighted in 1849, and "Mischief Polka" by C. H. W. (Carl Heinrich Weber, also known as C. Henry Weber), and the song "They Gathered Rose and the Stolen Heart" by Charlie Hine, copyrighted in 1850, all without plate numbers. The first plate numbers may not have been copyrighted. The earliest surviving Balmer & Weber publication is "Brattleboro Waltz & Quickstep" by George Hews, numbered 10 but not copyrighted. It is curious that the name of this good old Vermont town should turn up in Missouri and become attached to a waltz. The next surviving piece is number 18 and is not copyrighted. The composer is S. H. Seipp; the title "Love Not Quickstep."[5]

Balmer & Weber do not seem to have reprinted much important European music. There are no Haydn and Mozart sonatas. Beethoven's "Sonata Pathétique" came with one of the absorbed catalogs. The misattributed "Webster's Funeral March," a "Laendler," and a half-dozen waltzes that Beethoven never wrote disfigure the catalog. What a distorted view of Beethoven music lovers of this period must have had: on the one hand a few sonatas, and on the other these silly pieces that Beethoven would have been incapable of perpetrating. To be sure, these concoctions had been published by Germans and dutifully reprinted by Americans not so critical as they might have been.

Balmer & Weber reprinted many of the easy operatic transcriptions of Czerny, Brunner, Beyer, Dorn, Spindler,[6] and Burgmüller. They also reprinted many of the brilliant operatic fantasies of Sidney Smith, Franz Liszt, Eugene Ketterer, and Ignace Leybach. They were partial to the English songs of George Barker, Stephen Glover, Samuel Lover, Henry Bishop, as well as the German songs of Franz Abt, Franz Schubert, and Friedrich Kuecken.

It was to be expected that St. Louis would be amply represented in their catalog. The songs and piano pieces of P. G. Anton, Edward M. Bowman, Bernard A. Bode, R. Frank Cardella, August C. Eimer, Benjamin Owen, J. W. Postlewaite, the Robyns (Henry, William, and Alfred G.), Edouard Sobolewski, and August Waldauer were very much in evidence. The publication of a local composition was not always a noble gesture. Frequently a composer would be anxious to see himself in print and cheerfully pay for the privilege. Charles Balmer wrote so much that recourse was had to a number of pseudonyms. The usual ones were Charles Remlab (Balmer backwards), T. Van Berg, Alphonse Leduc, Charles Lange, Henry Werner, August Schumann, T. Mayer, and F. B. Ryder.

Did Balmer & Weber have their own engraver? There are not pieces enough available to be able to tell if they made use of the engraver that Nathaniel Phillips brought here to engrave his last fifteen pieces. There is evidence that Balmer & Weber had some of their early pieces engraved by George W. Quidor of New York City. In their time, Balmer & Weber did a tremendous business. They put St. Louis on the map as the publishing center of the country. Henry Weber died in Denver 6 September 1892, and Charles Balmer passed away in St. Louis the same year, December 15. After the death of the partners, the business was carried on by a company in which the Balmer family was strongly represented.

Lack of efficient leadership brought about a let-down in publishing activity. The rise of Shattinger, Thiebes-Stierlin, and Val Reis resulted in a decline in music sales that rendered advisable a discontinuance of the store on Olive Street. A significant inroad on the sale of publications was made by the aggressive policy of Kunkel Brothers. The Kunkel publication program was far in advance of that of Balmer & Weber and inevitably brought about its demise.

REFERENCE

Krohn, *Missouri Music* (New York: Da Capo, 1971).

------

5. [All in this paragraph, except the pieces by Weber, Hine, and Seipp, are at GML.]

6. [Fritz Spindler? This composer, but not operatic transcriptions, except for Wagner's "Tannhäuser's Marsch," listed in Keck's dissertation. —Ed.]

7

TO ENGRAVE OR NOT TO ENGRAVE

One of the questions involved in early publishing is that of the actual engraving and printing of the music. In 1820, when the *Missouri Harmony* was published, it carried a St. Louis imprint, although it was actually printed in Cincinnati. The music was not engraved, but typeset by a printer who had a font of music type. Most books of psalmody as well as most hymnbooks were typeset. Sheet music, on the other hand, was printed from engraved plates.

The engravers of sheet music could be divided into two classes: those who engraved title-pages, and those who engraved the actual music. Those who designed and engraved title-pages were normally copper-plate engravers who often included their names in the design. Those who engraved the music usually struck their names at the bottom of the last plate of music. Unfortunately, the practice of signing the title-page and last plate of music was by no means universal, so that it is only in relatively rare cases that we know who did the job.

There were music engravers in all of the large cities of the Atlantic seaboard before 1800. Only towards the end of the first half of the nineteenth century did music engravers and publishers penetrate the inner states. Louisville was fortunate in having a music engraver as early as 1842. However, it was not until 1845 that Jacob Slinglandt was recorded in the Louisville City Directory as "music engraver" at Peters. He had punches whose characteristics were unmistakable, and it is evident from sheet music available that he engraved practically everything that William Cummings Peters published in Louisville and Cincinnati. About half of the surviving publications are actually signed by him on the last plate of each piece. That Cincinnati did not have a music engraver in 1840 is evident from the score of "General Harrison's Grand March." Although the heading seems to have been engraved on the plate by an ordinary engraver and then transferred to the lithographic stone, the music is either hand-written on the stone or inscribed on manuscript paper and then transferred to the stone. "The Citizens Guards' March" was engraved by L. W. Webb of Baltimore.

Where was Draper's "St. Louis Grand March" (see Fig. 4 above, p. 16) engraved? Could we have had a music engraver in 1839? The very first City Directory, that of 1821, lists James Otis Lewis of 118 Main Street as an engraver. That he was a capable craftsman was proved by his portrait of Daniel Boone after the painting by Chester Harding. But did he have the tools required for music engraving? The same question could be raised in regard to the announcement in the *Missouri Republican* of 23 January 1839: "ENGRAVING: Door Plates, Trunk Plates, Coffin Plates, Dog Collars, Spoons, Jewelry, Umbrellas, Canes, etc., Neatly Engraved. Jewelers and others having engraving to be done, can be sure of having it executed with punctuality and on moderate terms at N. Phillips' Umbrella and Parasol Manufactory, 28 Market street." Such an engraver could engrave a title-page, but would he have the tools requisite for music engraving? These would include steel punches for treble and bass clefs, for black and white notes, for flats and sharps, rests, letters for *piano, mezzo, forte,* and other indications of loudness and softness, and the fluctuations of tempos. Would he be able to draw lined staffs on a metal plate and then punch the notation in reverse position on that plate? To be sure, there is the advertisement in the *Missouri Republican* for 1 January 1849, "The subscriber has the largest and most complete stock of standard music in the western country, to which he is making additions daily of his own publication--got up in his own establishment--Music and Military Store, 42 Market street." However, this is ten years later and Nathaniel Phillips may have imported a music engraver by that time.

his new publishing venture. It is true that we had at least one lithographer in St. Louis in 1839, Eugene Dupré of 66 Main Street, but Nathaniel may have deemed him not qualified for the task at hand. Not only that, but he would have to have the music engraved elsewhere, so why not have the whole job done there? "Oliver's Quick Step" by Nichols, arranged by B. A. Burditt,[1] had a somewhat similar lithograph on its title-page. The tents in the encampment were practically the same in both lithographs, and Old Glory flew from an improvised flagstaff to the right. This lithograph was designed by Bufford and printed at the Thayer Lithographic Establishment in Boston. The piece was published by Henry Prentiss of Boston, who held forth at Court Street from 1827 to 1847 and was absorbed by Ditson around 1847. It is just within the bounds of possibility that the lithograph in the first edition of "St. Louis Grand March" was designed by Bufford and printed in Boston. As for the engraving, the punches used in both editions of the "March" were practically identical with those used in the publications of Parker & Ditson, specifically in the song "When the Moonbeams Tender Light" by G. A. Hodson[2] and many others printed before 1840. There is one slight deviation. The treble clef used on the first page of the first edition of the "March" is slightly different from the treble clef used on the second page. This may have been due to the fact that in a busy shop like that of Parker & Ditson there may have been more than one set of tools. There may have been more than one engraver. There is little doubt that both editions of "St. Louis Grand March" were engraved and lithographed in Boston.

When Charles Balmer published his "St. Louis Firemen's Parade March" in 1842, he stated on the title-page "On stone by J. Erwin" and "Edw'd Hutawa, Lith'r, 7 S. Third, St. Louis." That meant that the design was drawn on the stone by J. Erwin, who was the artist. Then Edward Hutawa printed the title from that stone. J. Erwin is not listed in any City Directory. The Directory of 1842 lists Edward Hutawa as architect and surveyor at 7 S. Third Street. The Directory for 1842 carries a nine-line advertisement on plate 88 announcing "Edward Hutawa, Lithographic and Map Publishing Office, No. 8 S. Third street." It would be a logical step from surveying and drawing maps to printing them, provided that one had a lithographic stone and the requisite printing equipment. In the case of the Balmer opus, the engraved notes as well as the title-page were printed by lithography. The question still remains: where were the two pages of notes engraved? The clefs are really unique. The treble clef has a very heavy downstroke and a spidery upstroke. The bass clef is very thick and heavy. After examining innumerable compositions published between 1820 and 1850 in all of the centers of the East, I have not been able to match these punches. Nor were they used in any subsequent publications of Nathaniel or J. & J. R. Phillips. Could we have been visited by an itinerant engraver who engraved these plates and then departed for parts unknown?

The next Nathaniel publication, Woolcott's "St. Louis Quadrilles," was engraved in Boston, since it was published by George P. Reed and copyrighted by William H. Oakes, both of Boston. "Vive la Dance" and "The Hope Too Bright to Last" were undoubtedly engraved in Boston, for I have found a piano piece and a song, both engraved with the identical punches, one published by Henry Prentiss and the other by Oliver Ditson. The engraver was undoubtedly an itinerant operator who did work for both shops. "Mary Blane" is another mystery, for I have not been able to find similar punches anywhere. However, one must not forget that only an infinitesimal portion of the eastern output ever reached St. Louis. We do not have an adequate representation of our own output. Consider the publications of N. Phillips. It is difficult to believe that he published nothing between 1839 and 1847. More concretely, his plate number series reveal gaps. "A" has not survived in the alphabetical series, and 1-20, 22, 24, and 25 are missing in the numerical series.

---

1. [Copy at GML.]

2. [Copy at GML.]

In 1839, Nathaniel seems to have acquired an engraver, for the last surviving fifteen pieces are all engraved with the same tools. This would substantiate the statement previously quoted, "The subscriber has the largest stock of music . . . to which he is making additions daily of his own publications--*got up in his own establishment*" (the italics are mine). The intriguing mystery is this--if Nathaniel actually had an engraver, what became of him when Nathaniel sold his catalog to Balmer & Weber? Since too few of their early publications have survived, we cannot tell if they took him over to engrave their music.

It has not been my intention to discover the original engravers of the catalog of J. & J. R. Phillips. Every piece seems to have been done by a different hand. The fate of the J. & J. R. music is puzzling. While every one of Nathaniel's pieces can be accounted for in the Balmer & Weber catalog, those of J. & J. R. do not seem to have been integrated so soon.

The earliest dated Balmer & Weber print that has survived is "The Grand Hungarian Triumphal March," composed by Joseph Gungl and copyrighted in 1849.[3] It was engraved on two plates by George W. Quidor of New York City; his name is stamped on the second plate. The plates carry no plate number. Quidor's characteristic slanting treble clef appears on several subsequent pieces which may indicate that he engraved these pieces even though he failed to sign the plates.

The earliest signed title-page is that of "Winter Evening Waltz" by Charles Balmer, copyrighted in 1852.[4] The surviving copy is marked "new edition" and was engraved by J. Scharr, a local craftsman. It is barely possible that the first edition had no title-page or was engraved by another engraver. It may have been engraved on two plates with a heading.

---

3. [Copy at GML.]

4. [Copy at GML.]

Fig. 10. Louis Antoine Jullien, The Fireman's Quadrille (New York: Samuel C. Jollie, 1854), title-page

8

THE LITHOGRAPHED TITLE-PAGE

When Alois Senefelder began experimenting with the possibilities of lithography, he had no definite object in view. He eventually invented a new kind of ink that could be used on the lithographic stone. The stone originally came from Bavaria. Through the use of a new chemical formula, he found that he could reproduce anything that had been written with this ink. He had to teach himself the art of writing backwards so that the object on the stone would be properly reversed when imprinted on a sheet of paper.

The printing of music first suggested itself to him. In 1796, he actually printed a small edition of *Twelve Songs* that had been composed by his friend Gleissner. He next printed a "Duetto for Two Flutes" by the same Gleissner and then proceeded to print an "Ode on the Death of Mozart" by Cannabich. He finally developed a suitable technique for all types of lithography, not the least of which was the printing of title-pages for musical compositions.

The most notable period for the colored lithograph was from 1850 to 1880 when it fairly luxuriated. If it was desired to sell a new composition it was given a lurid title-page. Pieces that had achieved success were usually put forth with a collective title-page in black and white.

The tragedy of the colored title-page was that it aroused the cupidity of the collector. He frequently tore the title-page from the music and threw the music away. Collectors lost sight of the fact that the whole piece of music was important because of the copyright claim, the plate number, and the music itself.

To be sure, no masterpiece lurked behind a brilliant title-page, but the music was characteristic of the musical taste of the period. The majority of the music consisted of dance forms--polkas, waltzes, schottisches, redowas, quadrilles, marches, quicksteps, galops, with an occasion theme and variations thrown in to vary the monotony. The theme to be varied would usually be some popular operatic tune or "Home Sweet Home." No sonatas or other classical or romantic forms were common, although Meditations, Reveries, Nocturnes, Rondos, or Fantasies would be attempted.

The time will come when we will collect the complete works of a given composer such as Charles Grobe, whose opus numbers run rather high. Such men cannot be looked at with the same eyes with which we look at Chopin. These early American composers were the product of a particular stage of American culture and are of historical significance, but not musical.

In the middle of the century, St. Louis was one of the musical publishing centers of the United States. Consequently, we had more than our share of lithographers. Among the first-class lithographers may be mentioned Alexander McLean, E. & G. Robyn & Company, R. P. Studley & Company, and R. J. Compton & Company. When these firms became overloaded we frequently had recourse to J. H. Bufford & Company of Boston, Saroni, Major, & Knapp of New York, or Ehrgott & Forbiger of Cincinnati. Outstanding artists in St. Louis were J. Erwin and L. Pomarede.

The designers of title-pages had a few conventions to comply with. The simplest way to design a title-page was to draw the picture first and fit in the lettering afterward, being careful not to destroy the artistic balance of the picture. The lettering usually consisted of the title of the piece, the composer of the music, and if a song the author of the words. At the bottom of the page would be placed the name of the publisher and the names of secondary publishers who would act as sales agents in other localities. Somewhere room would be found for the symbol indicating the price.

Portraits were usually drawn within a circle with the lettering above and below the circle. The portrait was frequently in profile. Since the cover was tall and narrow, an oval was used more frequently. This would accommodate a full-length figure or a group of figures. When buildings were drawn on a title-page they could have historical significance. Hotels, court houses, theater buildings or opera houses, stores, and schools very frequently found their way onto a title-page design. One of the most striking of title-pages produced anywhere was Jullien's "The Fireman's Quadrille" that depicted the burning of the Crystal Palace in New York with the lurid red and yellow of the fire, creating a most dramatic effect (Fig. 10). A somewhat similar cover was printed of the burning of the Southern Hotel in St. Louis, but a copy is not available for illustration. Since St. Louis is a river city, Mississippi steamboats were frequently depicted in characteristic positions. These pictures of river boats have historic significance, for they are frequently the only pictures extant of the boats involved. The vast majority of piano pieces published were of the commonly accepted dance forms. There were no reprints of sonatas or other classical or romantic forms. There were no reprints of Chopin or Schumann.

In the vocal field, the situation was slightly different. There were collections of oratorio songs that brought in Handel, Haydn, Mozart, and Mendelssohn. It is amazing how many songs were published. The vocal teachers of the time must have had a lucrative time teaching their students all of the songs that emanated from the presses of Balmer & Weber. This was the era of the opera stock companies when you could get a good seat for fifty cents and see a different opera every night. Consequently there were many songs from the operas. This was also the period of the ubiquitous operatic transcriptions of Ferdinand Beyer, Charles Brunner, and Heinrich Dorn.[1]

---

1. [There is an entry for Heinrich Dorn (1804-92) in *Baker's*. However, George Keck's dissertation lists only music by an Edouard Dorn. —Ed.]

9

PLATE NUMBERS

It is customary for a publisher to make a record of his publications. Sometimes the record is kept alphabetically by composers; sometimes it is listed by titles. The usual procedure is to assign a number to each publication.[1] John Walsh of London began to number his publications about 1730.[2] These numbers are usually called plate numbers because the number is stamped at the bottom of every plate. If a number is assigned to each piece of music as it is printed, the record will be in numerical order as well as in chronological succession. If the record is kept in numerical order and every piece is dated by its copyright claim, the record will be practically perfect. But such perfection is not for ordinary humans, and there will come a time when the publisher will become careless or in too much of a hurry to keep the record straight. Then there will come a time when pieces are not published, whereas the record would seem to indicate they had been. Should an entry not be dated, its position in the chronological sequence may be ascertained by reference to adjoining numbers that are dated.

About half of the early American publishers used plate numbers. Some used the alphabet A to Z and AA to ZZ, but this proved too clumsy and was soon abandoned.[3] At least one publisher used a new number for every plate. As a result, a given publication would have a group of numbers. This proved too cumbersome and was soon given up. The idea of using a single number for a whole composition eventually became common practice. Those publishers who did not use plate numbers engraved the title of the piece at the bottom of each plate. If a composi-

---

1. W. Barclay Squire, in 1914, referred to them as "publishers' numbers." More recently, Richard J. Wolfe referred to them as "plate numbers" if each plate received an individual number. If each composition received a number, regardless of the number of plates involved, he named them "publication numbers." In this essay, "plate number" is to be understood as referring to a number for each composition. See W. B. Squire, "Publishers' Numbers," *Sammelbände der internationalen Musikgesellschaft* 15 (1913-14): 420-27; R. S. Hill, "The Plate Numbers of C. F. Peters Predecessors," *Papers of the American Musicological Society* (1938), 113-34; K. Meyer, "Artaria Plate Numbers," *Notes*, series 1, no. 5 (December 1942): 1-22; C. E. Deutsch, *Music Publishers' Numbers* (London, 1946); A. Weinman, *Vollständiges Verlagsverzeichniss Artaria & Comp.* (Vienna, 1952); R. Elvers, "Datierte Verlagsnummern Berliner Musik Verleger," in *Festschrift O. E. Deutsch* (Kassel, 1963), 291-95; O. W. Neighbour and A. Tyson, *English Music Publishers' Plate Numbers* (London, 1965).

2. See W. C. Smith, *A Bibliography of the Musical Works Published by John Walsh during the Years 1695-1720* (London, 1948), xxii; also W. C. Smith and C. Humphries, *A Bibliography of the Musical Works Published by the Firm of John Walsh during the Years 1721-1766* (London, 1968), xiv-xv.

3. See "Publisher's Plate and Publication Numbering Systems" in R. J. Wolfe, *Secular Music in America, 1801-1825: A Bibliography*, 3 vols. (New York, 1964), 3:1181-1200, especially p. 1187. [See also Wolfe, *Early American Music Engraving and Printing: A History of Music Publishing in America from 1787 to 1825 with Commentary on Earlier and Later Practices* (Urbana, 1980). —Ed.]

tion was to be reprinted it would be helpful to know how many plates constituted the whole piece. Some publishers began to add a digit after the title; the digit indicated the number of plates required for the complete piece. Then some publishers began to engrave the plate number, followed by the title, followed by the digit.

In 1846, Henry J. Peters & Company engraved at the bottom of three plates "Shelbyville Waltz 164-4." By the simple expedient of dropping the title arrives a formula that would completely identify the piece. So we find the same Peters, in 1847, using "132 3." In 1848, W. C. Peters & Company used 177-3; in 1849, Peters, Webb & Company used 136-3; in 1850, Balmer & Weber used 137=3; in fact, they may have used 46=2 in 1848. After H. J. Peters started the hyphenated numbering, all of his western colleagues followed his example.

To what extent did eastern publishers use the hyphenated system? An examination of over five hundred eastern imprints revealed the fact that in the period 1820 to 1853 about a dozen eastern publishers used plate numbers. Of particular importance were F. D. Benteen; Oliver Ditson; A. Fiot; Firth & Hall; Firth, Hall, & Pond; Firth, Pond, & Company; William Hall & Son; Hewitt & Jacques; Lee & Walker; Leopold Meignen; George Reed & Company; and George Willig, Jr. The practice among these was by no means uniform. Some published as many pieces without as with. Among all these publishers only Lee & Walker of Philadelphia used the hyphenated system. In 1846, they published the "Ravel Polka" by Matthias Keller with the number 213.2.[4] By 1860, 8167.5 had been reached. It will be noticed that they used a period instead of a hyphen. An 1852 issue of George Willig, Jr. has survived, properly marked 2489-3. By the time Balmer & Weber took this up, they used a double hyphen (=). It is just possible that hyphenated plate numbering originated in the Middle West, and that Lee & Walker picked it up from Peters' publications available in Baltimore since 1844.

---

4. [Copy at GML.]

10

THE PETERS FAMILY

The name Peters is a resounding one in the musical world. The American Peters stems from William Smalling Peters, who came from England in 1820 with a family consisting of two girls and three boys. His eldest son, William Cummings, was born in Devonshire on 10 March 1805. The next son, Henry J., was a mere child when they emigrated, having been born in 1816. The third son, John, need not detain us here, for he strayed into shoemaking. At different times the Peters were in Pittsburgh, Louisville, and Cincinnati. William Cummings had three sons, all of whom entered the musical field. John L., Alfred C., and William M. were all American-born and followed faithfully in their father's footsteps.

John L. and Alfred C. seem to have started a music business at St. Louis in the 1850s. A piano piece, "Miss Lucy Long," with variations by W. Striby, was entered for copyright in the District Court of Eastern Missouri by J. L. Peters in 1851. Their first entry in the St. Louis Directory was in that of 1859 when they were located at 49 Fifth Street. From about 1851 to 1867 the firms of A. C. Peters & Brother of Cincinnati and J. L. Peters & Brother of St. Louis seem to have been one and the same firm. The imprint on the title-pages usually reads A. C. Peters & Brother--Cincinnati, or J. L. Peters & Brother--St. Louis.

In order to be on the safe side, it may be wise to cite the titles of their productions that carry a Missouri imprint. They are, for 1851, "Miss Lucy Long" (already noted), "Dixey's Reel" by Alfred de St. Julien; for 1866, "Sérénade à Marie" by Charles Kinkel,[1] "Love's Chidings Polka" by Julius Becht, "Shells of the Ocean" by F. Rudolphson, "Belle Fena Mazurka" by Laurence Grannis,[2] "Martha" arranged for four hands by C. Berger, "Then You'll Remember Me" from Balfe's *Bohemian Girl*, transcribed by Charles Grobe, "Moss Rose," "Japan Rose," "White Rose," "Monthly Rose," "China Rose," all waltzes by J. P. Coupa, "Pretty Blue Forget Me Not" by Charles Kinkel, and "Write a Letter from Home" by A. Paoler.[3]

From 1856 to 1859, John L. and Alfred C. were part of the firm of W. C. Peters & Sons of Cincinnati. In 1866, John L. opened a store in New York City. He was at 200 North Broadway in 1866, at 198 Broadway in 1868-69, 599 Broadway from 1870 to 1874, and at 1843 Broadway in 1875. He sold his New York sheet music business to Oliver Ditson in 1877.

In 1867, J. L. Peters bought the stock and catalog of H. M. Higgins of Chicago. He presumably had the plates shipped to St. Louis. The sheet music and musical merchandise were sold to the De Motte Brothers of Chicago, who transferred everything to their Chicago store at 91 Washington Street. However, within a year they sold the same stock back to J. L. Peters, who shipped everything to his New York store at 599 Broadway.

---

1. [The spelling "Kinkel" is not an error for Kunkel (see chapter 15). George Keck reports that 41 pieces by Charles Kinkel are at the GML, all published during the period of Kunkel and by the same publishers; but asks if perhaps Kinkel is a pseudonym for Kunkel? —Ed.]

2. [Corrected from Krohn's "La Feen Mazurka" by George Keck.]

3. [At GML: "Miss Lucy Long," "Sérénade à Marie," "Shells of the Ocean," "Belle Fena Mazurka," "Then You'll Remember Me."]

The St. Louis address of J. L. Peters was at 212 North Fifth Street from 1859 to 1871. In 1869, the firm name was changed to J. L. Peters & Company, the "company" being T. August Boyle. While Peters was in New York, Boyle conducted the St. Louis business. A published survival is the song "Only a Little Flower" by F. Pannell, issued in 1870.

Peters seems to have returned to St. Louis in 1881. He was located at 307 North Fifth Street (Broadway) from 1881 to 1885. Several piano pieces have survived from this period. For 1882 we have "Emma's Delight Waltz" by Florence Percy; five 1883 copyrights, "Sweet Dreams" by August Rosen, a piano duet "Merry Cousins," "Water Witch: Valse Brillante" by Oscar Werner, "Distant Bells" by Edwin Christie, and "Heavenly Chimes" by Charles Kinkel. There are four 1884 copyrights: "Sunny South Polka" by M. Graziani, "Rippling Waters" by August Pacher, and two songs, "Go Ask the Roses" by Edwin Christie and "Hush Thee My Baby" by Arthur Sullivan, arranged by A. R. Richards. Finally for 1885, we have another song, "You Had Better Ask Me" by M. Louis.

In 1886 Peters moved his store to 1011 Olive Street, in 1887 to 1102 Olive Street, in 1890 to 224 North Fourth Street, and in 1892 to 822 Olive Street. This is the last directory entry, and he may well have closed up shop by then. The date of his death is not known.

11

ST. LOUIS AND THE STAR SPANGLED BANNER

When Francis Scott Key wrote the first draft of "The Defence of Fort M'Henry," he had in mind a contemporary English drinking song that had been composed in the 1770s by John Stafford Smith for the Anacreontic Society in London. The tune became very popular and was used for a number of American patriotic songs, of which "For the Glorious Fourteenth of July" (1797), "Adams and Liberty" (1798), and "The Battle of the Wabash" (1812) are good examples. The first publication of the words and music, now called "The Star Spangled Banner," by the Carrs in Baltimore in 1814 required two engraved plates.

This is number 1 in Joseph Muller's bibliography *The Star Spangled Banner: Words and Music Issued between 1814 and 1864*, published in 1935. At the bottom of the first plate was engraved "(Adapd & Arr'd by T. C.)," which indicates that the music had been edited by Thomas Carr, the son of Joseph Carr, the publisher. It was not until 1819 that Joseph bequeathed his publishing business to his son Thomas. The music was notated in the key of C, the melody in the right hand and the bass part in the left hand. A few chords were inserted here and there for emphasis, but it could not be said that it was harmonized. The next six editions of "The Star Spangled Banner" were all reissues of the Carr edition. They are listed by Muller as numbers 2 to 7.

The first harmonized edition was published by Firth & Hall, New York, in the early 1830s. The chords are rather simple, the harmony alternating between C and G. The second harmonized edition was published and copyrighted in 1843 by Joseph F. Atwill of New York. It was published as one of six patriotic songs arranged by Francis H. Brown. "The Star Spangled Banner" was transposed to B-flat and the harmonization abounds in octaves and heavy chords. The third harmonization was published by Oliver Ditson in 1848; this is Muller's number 21. It somewhat resembles the Firth & Hall recension.

The fourth harmonized version was published in St. Louis in 1852 by John L. Peters & Brother, the brother probably being Alfred C. Peters. The editorial work, including the arranging of the chorus for four voices, was done by C. Merkley, a virtually unknown local musician. This was the smoothest and musically the best of the harmonized editions. It is numbered 25 in Muller's bibliography. W. C. Peters & Sons of Cincinnati either borrowed or bought the J. L. Peters plates from which they published an edition in 1856. This is listed number 31 by Muller. Using the same plates, Alfred C. Peters & Brother, also of Cincinnati, got out their edition in 1864; this is Muller 31c.

J. L. Peters & Brother of St. Louis apparently recovered their original plates from which they printed another edition in 1866. Since Oliver Ditson & Company of Boston bought the Peters catalog in 1870, Ditson issued another edition sometime in the 1870s.

A few deviations in the text characterize the Peters plates. Most of these changes were made elsewhere before 1852. The omission of "broad" occurred first in the Cole edition, Muller 7. "'Mid the havoc" was first introduced in the Atwill edition, number 15. Atwill also used "They'd leave us no more." "Oh!" instead of plain "O" first appeared in the Firth & Hall edition, number 8. "Gave proof through the night" is to be found in the A. C. Bacon & Company edition, number 2. George Willig saw fit to phrase it "praise the power" in number 6. Otherwise, the words are the same as those used by Carr in the first edition. Merkley notated the music in 3/4 meter instead of 6/4. This improvement had been made in the Cole edition.

The use of the J. L. Peters plates in four additional editions poses several baffling problems. No copy of the original 1852 Peters edition has survived. Consequently we do not know the exact position of the copyright claim, nor do we know of the location of a plate number. The J. L. Peters reprint of 1866 shows plate number 1812.3. This could not have been the original plate number for the simple reason that by 1866 the earliest number was 581. When W. C. Peters used the original plates, he entered the copyright claim for 1856 as well as his plate number 1398. To do this he had to obliterate the entire "J. L. Peters" and punch in his own claim.

A. C. Peters seems to have felt the need of a new copyright claim, but he printed his claim on the title-page. Muller does not mention whether the first plate of music still carried the claim of W. C. Peters. When J. L. Peters recovered his plates, he recopyrighted his edition as of 1866. To do this he would have to obliterate the claim of W. C. Peters and punch in his own. This could have been the time that he inserted his own plate number 1812.3. The manner in which it is squeezed in between the copyright claim and the lowest line of music indicates clearly that he was having trouble with the elimination of the W. C. Peters claim and the re-engraving of his own. Did Ditson eliminate Peters' 1866 entry and substitute 1852, or did Peters do that before he sold the plates to Ditson?

Why all this recopyrighting? J. L. Peters' original copyright was only valid for the arrangement by Merkley. He could not copyright "The Star Spangled Banner" because that was public property. What did W. C. and A. C. Peters have to copyright in their issues of 1856 and 1864? It was logical for J. L. Peters to recopyright his edition of 1866, for that would reaffirm the validity of his original copyright in 1852. Ditson apparently relied on this 1852 copyright because he did not recopyright the 1870 edition in his own name.

Balmer & Weber published an edition of "The Star Spangled Banner" that is an almost exact copy of the edition published by John Cole of Baltimore in 1825. This is Muller's number 7. George Willig, Jr. used the Cole plates for his edition of 1839-41, Muller's 13. The Balmer & Weber edition may be dated 1854. It is not copyrighted, but carries the plate number 617.[1] The Balmer & Weber plate numbers for 1854 run from 607 to 641. Although the musical text, with one exception, is an exact copy of the Cole edition, the poetic text is not. The one musical exception is the G in the bass of the fourth measure, which is a quarter note with no compensating rest. This proves that this note was carelessly copied. The deviations in the text are: line 1, "Oh!" and "dawn's"; line 5, "rocket's"; 9, "mist"; 10, "foe's"; 12, "discloses"; 13, "morning's"; 18, "'Mid the havoc" and "battle's"; 19, "They'd leave us" and "more!"; 16, 24, 32, "and home of the brave"; 26, "war's"; and 27, "blest with vic'try."

Jacob Endres seems to have published an edition of "The Star Spangled Banner" in the 1860s. At least it is listed on the collective title-page of the vocal duet by Mendelssohn, "I Would that My Love." This piece was not copyrighted, but it carries the plate number 25. Since plate number 27 was published in 1860 and number 29 in 1859, it is just possible that "The Star Spangled Banner" of Endres was published in 1860. The Misses McDeavit and Wright of Washington, D.C. owned a copy published by Compton & Doan. In the 1940s they sold their collection to the Free Library of Philadelphia. In the course of the transaction, the copy disappeared. It may well have been a reprint of the earlier edition of Jacob Endres whose plates passed into the possession of Endres & Compton in 1865, of R. J. Compton in 1866, and Compton & Doan in 1867. Lester S. Levy and James J. Fuld included it in the list they published in *Notes* in 1970.

REFERENCES

The fascinating story of the origin of the music as well as the poem is related with genial expertness by Oscar George Sonneck in his book *The Star Spangled Banner* published by the Library of Congress in 1914 [and reprinted by Da Capo in 1969. See also Joseph Muller, *The Star Spangled Banner: Words and Music Issued between 1814-1864* (New York, 1935; reprint,

---

1. [Copy at GML.]

New York: Da Capo, 1973). For the attribution of the melody to John Stafford Smith, see William Lichtenwanger, "The Music of 'The Star Spangled Banner': From Ludgate Hill to Capitol Hill," *Quarterly Journal of the Library of Congress* 34, no. 3 (July 1977): 136-70, reprinted (slightly revised) as "The Music of 'The Star-Spangled Banner': Whence and Whither?" in *College Music Symposium* 18, no. 2 (fall 1978): 34-81. See also Lichtenwanger, "Richard S. Hill and 'The "Unsettled" Text of *The Star Spangled Banner*'," in *Richard S. Hill: Tributes from Friends*, ed. Carol June Bradley and James B. Coover, Detroit Studies in Music Bibliography, 58 (Detroit: Information Coordinators [now Harmonie Park Press in Warren, Mich.], 1987). —Ed.]

12

WILLIAM FODEN AND THE UBIQUITOUS GUITAR

The Italian and the Spanish guitar were popular social instruments in the colonial era. Not only did George Washington buy guitar strings for his niece, but Benjamin Franklin offered to teach guitar playing to the mother of Leigh Hunt. The talented composer Francis Hopkinson promised to sing to his fiancée Nancy Borden a newly composed song with guitar accompaniment. Where, in the days gone by, a love-sick gallant would serenade his lady love with a flute solo, he now would sing an amorous ditty to the accompaniment of his guitar.

The early French settlers in St. Louis were addicted to the violin, but with the advent of the English and German immigrants at the turn of the century the guitar put in its appearance. Its portability was all in its favor and it made chordal music available in situations in which a piano would never be possible.

So early as the 1790s, songs were published in the east with guitar accompaniment. The earliest American publication for guitar solo may well have been *The Philadelphia Pocket Companion for the Guitar or Clarinet*, issued by the Carrs of Philadelphia in 1794. The earliest guitar piece published in St. Louis may have been the "Melange for the Guitar" composed by Carl Gottwalt Weber and put forth by Balmer & Weber around 1854, for it carries the plate number 648. Carl Gottwalt had arranged guitar accompaniments for the songs "Maid of the Mill," "My Bonnie Kate," "Silken Bands," and "My Thoughts of Thee," published by W. C. Peters in Louisville. Carl Heinrich Weber, the brother of Gottwalt, contrived guitar accompaniments for the songs "On the Banks of the Old Salt River," "Vesper Hymn to the Virgin," and "It Is the Hour of Love," also published by Peters.

An early listing on the back of "Wait for the Waggon" by Charles Balmer (1851)[1] yields the titles of these guitar songs: "A Heart That's Kind and True" by Balmer, "Lela" by W. L. Hargrave, "The Zephyr's Choice" by C. Hine, "Jutie" by W. W. Rossington, "Can This Be Love?," "Farewell if Ever Fondest Prayer," "I'll Roam the Dewy Bowers" by C. G. Weber, and "Oh! Chide Me Not" by A. H. Lanphear as arranged by F. Nennstiel.[2] An exceedingly scarce Balmer & Weber catalog of 1894 lists over one hundred and fifty songs with guitar accompaniment.

Listings of guitar solo pieces include "Two German Waltzes" by J. Amann, "Bavarian Schottische" and "St. Louis Serenading Waltz" by Charles Balmer, "Narcissa Waltz No. 2" by T. B. Bishop, "Pandora March" by Charles Drumheller, "Dwelle March" and "Emily Waltz" by Charles Jenkins, "Au Revoir Waltz," "Forest Echo March," "Prairie Flower Fandango," and "Troubador's Serenade" by Lynde, "The Letter That Never Came" by Paul Dresser, "Had I the Choosing," "Manzanillo," and "Answer" by A. G. Robyn, and "Lincoln's Funeral March" by Schumann.

H. Pilcher & Sons, located at 91 North Fourth Street, published in 1857 a number of pieces by T. Brigham Bishop, the noted guitarist. These include the songs "I Stood on the Shore," "Come Be Queen of the Forest," as well as "Violet Polka," and "Celebrated Guitar Waltz." Additional guitar titles may be culled from the title-page of "Violet Polka," notably "Grand Waltz," "Gipsy Polka," "Fourth Street Galop," "The Last Rose of Summer," "My Heart and Lute,"

---

1. [Copy at GML.]

2. [This last piece is not listed on "Wait for the Waggon," according to Richard D. Wetzel. —Ed.]

and "Narcissa Waltz" nos. 1 and 2. The title-page of "I Stood on the Shore" yields the titles "Adella Maine," "Mary's Away," "Indian's Lament," and "The Wild Wood Birds." "The Hoop Polka" by Madame L. Picot bears the St. Louis imprint of Pilcher, but was actually copyrighted by Oliver Ditson Company in 1857.

The fact that Adam Shattinger was an accomplished guitar player may account for the publication of much guitar music in his catalog. Shattinger himself composed and published a transcription of Arditi's "Il Bacio," as well as some selections from *La Grande Duchesse de Gerolstein*, the popular operetta of Jacques Offenbach. Shattinger's greatest achievement was the publication in 1881 of *The School of the Guitarist*, a folio volume of exercises and pieces by William O. Bateman, the noted lawyer. Music was Bateman's recreation and avocation, for he not only composed but he also taught guitar and music engraving.

Bateman's early compositions were published by Lee & Walker of Philadelphia. They include "Aurora Waltz" (1849), "Sylvanus Waltz" (1851), "Brandywine Polka," and "Cracovienne Variations," none of which was copyrighted. "Brandywine Polka" was dedicated to Mary Powell, who was then located at the Public Library. In 1876, Kunkel Brothers published "Elf Queen Mazurka" and "Idyl." Shattinger copyrighted "Like a Rainbow" from *Il Trovatore* in 1877, "Dream of Von Weber" in 1879, and "Souvenir de Aguado Waltz" in 1880. Most of the pieces that Shattinger published were copyrighted as part of *The School of the Guitarist* in 1881. Among these may be mentioned "March of Croisez," "Tarantulla," "Forgotten Polka," "Philomela Waltz," "Beethoven's Dream Waltz," "Von Weber's Last Waltz," "Call Me Thine Own" from *L'Éclair* by Halévy, and two pieces from *Il Trovatore*, "Soldier's Chorus" and "Home to Our Mountains." All of these pieces were published separately. The Missouri Historical Society has manuscripts of "Shaker's Dance" and "Sweet Whispers Mazurka" which may not have been published. Bateman wrote a thirty-six page pamphlet *Harmonometry, or Science of Music and Musical Composition, Founded upon the Natural Progressions of Harmonic Sounds*, which was published by W. F. Dufy of Philadelphia in 1867.

Bateman's best pupil was William C. Foden. Foden was born in St. Louis on 23 March 1860. At age seven he began taking violin lessons. By sixteen he had become so capable a musician that he could conduct a small orchestra. Hearing a schoolmate play a guitar, he was so strongly attracted to that instrument that he resolved to study it seriously. His father bought him an old German instrument and procured a teacher. Within a year he was with Bateman and making rapid progress. In 1887 he became a member of a professional trio consisting of guitar, violin, and flute. He organized the Beethoven Mandolin and Guitar Orchestra, but soon altered the name to the Foden Mandolin and Guitar Orchestra, because it was recruited entirely from his own students. He next assembled a Guitar Quintet for which he had to compose and arrange suitable music. For eighteen years he taught at the Beethoven Conservatory of Music, and for seven years at Strassberger's Conservatory of Music. For fifteen years he coached the mandolin and guitar clubs at Smith Academy, a preparatory school for boys going to Washington University.

In 1904 Foden participated in the Third Annual Convention of the American Guild of Banjoists, Mandolinists, and Guitarists, playing in a Grand Concert on January at Carnegie Hall in New York City. The music journal *Cadenza* reviewed his playing in its February 1904 issue. Among other things it stated that "One is at a loss to find words to describe Foden's playing. He is more than a virtuoso. He executes trills, runs, tremolo passages, intricate chord combinations and sustained passages with a clearness of technique and fullness of tone usually associated with the harp." In 1911, at another Guild Convention, he functioned as soloist along with Giuseppe Pettina, mandolinist, and Frederick J. Bacon, banjoist. The three decided to join forces and tour the country. In order to be closer to Bacon, who lived in Vermont, and Pettina, who lived in Rhode Island, Foden decided to move to New York. In the fall of 1911 and the spring of 1912, they toured the country, giving forty-six concerts ranging from Boston to Vancouver, Los Angeles, Denver, St. Louis, Chicago, and New York. In reviewing the initial concert in Boston, *Crescendo* termed Foden the greatest guitarist in the country and marvelled at his three-finger tremolo and his beautiful tone.

Foden transcribed many songs, among them "Alice Where Art Thou," "Don't Forget to Write Me Darling," "Listen to the Mocking Bird," "Believe Me if All Those Endearing Young

Charms," "Home Sweet Home," "Annie Laurie," and the Foster songs "Old Black Joe," "Massa's in the Cold, Cold Ground," and "My Old Kentucky Home." He also wrote "A Grand Fantasie on American Songs." His operatic transcriptions include the "Sextette" from *Lucia*, and selections from Flotow's *Martha*, Weber's *Der Freischütz*, *Il Trovatore*, Auber's *Fra Diavolo*, and Wallace's *Maritana*. Favorite instrumental pieces were not neglected, so that we have Lange's "Flower Song," Moszkowski's "Serenata," Delibes's "Pizzicato," Boccherini's "Minuet," Mendelssohn's "Spring Song," and Dollman's "Convent Bells" in two versions.

While in New York, Foden composed three original compositions, ten song transcriptions, and a *Grand Method for the Guitar* in two volumes, all of which were published by William J. Smith & Company. J. C. Groene of Cincinnati published three songs, "Dark Blue Eyes," "Do Not Forget Me," and "Lighthouse by the Sea," as well as four solos and two duets. For Siegel-Myers Music School, a correspondence course in Chicago, he composed six easy pieces and ten more difficult solos.

Foden probably published many more pieces that have not survived or are not listed on collective title-pages. Many of his pieces were rescored for two guitars or for mandolin and guitar. For his guitar quintet he had to arrange or compose music for five guitars. The majority of his pieces were published in St. Louis under his own copyright claim. His greatest creation was his "Sonata for Guitar," which he began in 1904 and finished in 1941. It does not seem to have been published, although the manuscript was preserved in the collection of George Krick.

Foden's best pupil was George Krick. Krick taught in Philadelphia where he founded the Germantown School of Music. He came to St. Louis where he taught until his final illness. He died 3 April 1962. He does not seem to have done much composition. He amassed a fine library which has now become part of Gaylord Music Library.

REFERENCES

V. O. Bickford, "The Guitar in America," *Guitar Review* 22 (June 1959): 17-19.

A. C. Hoskins, "William Foden," *Guitar Review* 22 (June 1959): 22.

G. C. Krick, "Reminiscences of Wm. Foden," *Guitar Review* 22 (June 1959): 23.

G. Pettine, "Foden as I Knew Him," *Guitar Review* 22 (June 1959): 23.

C. Simpson, "Some Early American Guitarists," *Guitar Review* 22 (June 1959): 16.

J. Zuth, *Handbuch der Laute und Gitarre* (Vienna, 1926), 101.

13

THE COMPTON COMPLEX

It may have been in the spring of 1832 that John Compton and his wife Ann Jordan Compton left their home in County Kent, England, crossed the Atlantic, and settled in the thriving city of Buffalo in the state of New York. On November 9 of the same year their son Richard Jordan was born. John Compton died of the cholera in 1841 and his wife was left with several young children to raise. At age eleven, Richard went to Grand Rapids, Michigan, to live with some friends, the Stanfords. Within a few years he was back in Buffalo and eventually became an engraver and lithographer. He is so recorded in the directories from 1849 to 1856. By 1853 he had established his own business, Compton & Company. The next year he entered into partnership with Charles Gibson as Compton & Gibson. By 1856 he sold his entire interest in the business to John Sage & Sons. He had married Ella Louise Cleveland[1] in 1853, and by 1856 decided to move his family to St. Louis.[2]

Compton began modestly enough in St. Louis as an engraver of silverplate, working in his own shop from 1857 to 1864.[3] By 1865, he had entered into partnership with Jacob Endres for the manufacture of pianos, their shops being located at 262-264 and 354-356 Market Street.[4] During 1866-67, he functioned as president of the St. Louis Piano Manufacturing Company with offices at 42 North Fourth Street, and a factory at Fifth and Papin in 1866, and 205 North Fourth Street and 837-839 South Fifth in 1867.[5] The St. Louis Piano Manufacturing Company acquired a new president in 1868, and Compton entered into partnership with Thomas C. Doan. As Compton & Doan they did some music publishing with headquarters at 205 North Fourth Street and 204 North Fifth Street.[6]

From 1870 to 1872, Compton functioned as foreman and superintendent of the lithographic department of R. P. Studley & Company at 221 North Main Street.[7] At some time along the line he was associated with the Globe Lithographing Company.[8] During 1873 and 1874 he acted as president of the Democrat Lithographing and Printing Company at Fourth and Pine.[9] As Compton & Dry he published a large volume entitled *Pictorial St. Louis: The Great*

---

1. See Mildred Cleveland, *Cleveland-Compton Families* (Chambersburg, Penn., 1941).

2. Directory entries abstracted by the Buffalo Public Library.

3. Entries in St. Louis city directories from 1837 to 1864.

4. Entry in City Directory for 1865.

5. Entry for city directories for 1866 and 1867.

6. Entry in City Directory for 1868 and imprint on sheet music.

7. Entry in city directories for 1870 and 1872.

8. See Cleveland, *Cleveland-Compton Families*.

9. Entry in city directories for 1873 and 1874.

Metropolis of the Mississippi Valley.[10]   This is an elaborate description of St. Louis with drawings, pictures, and maps.

By 1877, Compton was manager of the St. Louis Lithographing & Printing Company.[11] For three years, 1879 to 1881, he was president of the Compton Label Works located at 423 North Third Street.[12] From 1882 to 1887 he served as president of the Compton Lithographing Company with his son Richard Jordan, Jr., established as bookkeeper.[13] The title of the firm changed to Compton & Sons Lithographing and Printing Company in 1888.[14] The sons involved were Richard Jordan, Jr., George B., Paul, and Palmer Cleveland. Richard Jordan Compton, Sr. died 20 May 1898 at the age of sixty-six years.[15]

Compton was always known as a "public spirited citizen." He was one of the original members of the Merchants Exchange and of the Fall Festivities Association. He participated in the development of the Veiled Prophet Ball and Procession. Mrs. Compton suggested using the mysterious character the Veiled Prophet of Khorassan, taken from Thomas Moore's famous poem *Lalla Rookh*. Compton took an active interest in the annual St. Louis Exposition held in the St. Louis Music and Exposition Hall, a commodious building at Fourteenth and Olive Street that preceded the present public library building. He was also a supporter of the Wayman Crow Art Museum at Nineteenth and Locust. He was senior warden at St. Peter's Episcopal Church for many years, and was also a prominent Mason, a Knight Templar, and a member of the Legion of Honor, the A.O.U.W., and the Woodmen of the World.[16]

After Compton's death his sons carried on the lithographic business. George B. Compton[17] was elected president in 1904 of Compton & Sons, Inc., at 10645 Baur Boulevard.[18]

Jacob Endres seems to have started publishing at 52 Fourth Street before Richard J. Compton. Fortunately, his plate number 1 has survived. It happens to be "Pike's Peak March" by Gustav Baumhauer (Fig. 11), embellished with a view of Pike's Peak that looks like an inverted ice cream cone![19] Plate number 3 is a song "Cora Lyle" by P. G. Anton, "Professor of Music, Terre Haute Female College," with words by Clarence May. Within the capital "C" on the title-page is pictured a crude engraving of a May Pole Dance.[20] "I Would that My Love" is a duet by Felix Mendelssohn to a poem by Heinrich Heine.[21] It was provided with a collective title-page

---

10. Copy in MHS.

11. Entry in city directories for 1877 and 1878.

12. Entry in city directories for 1879, 1880, 1881.

13. Entries in city directories from 1882 to 1887.

14. Directory listing for 1888.

15. Date furnished by Britton A. Compton.

16. Data supplied by Clarence A. Spaethe of Compton & Sons.

17. See *The Book of St. Louisans*, 2nd ed. (St. Louis, 1912), 127-28.

18. See *St. Louis Telephone Directory*, August 1970, p. 262.

19. Copy in Mercantile Library and GML; title-page + 3 plates.

20. Copy in GML; title-page + 3 plates, copyrighted 1859.

21. Copy in GML; title-page + 5 plates numbered 25; no copyright claim.

Fig. 11. Gustav Baumhauer, Pike's Peak March (St. Louis: Jacob Endres, 1859), title-page

Compton

headed "Old and New, a Collection of Songs and Duetts," from which it is possible to glean many titles that have not survived:

Annie Laurie
Bobbin Round
Il Bacio
A Dollar or Two
Home, Sweet Home
Katy Darling
My Happy Home
Kathleen Mavourneen
Star Spangled Banner
When the Swallows Homeward Fly
I Cannot Dance Tonight
Shells of Ocean, by Cherry
My Home, by J. H. Doppler
Valley of Chamouni
Ever of Thee
Within a Mile of Edinboro Town
May Breezes
Ave Maria
Goodnight, Farewell, by Kuecken
Thou Art Gone from My Gaze
My Mother Dear
Mary of Argyle
Spring and Love
Mother Is the Battle Over
Her Bright Smile
Image of the Rose
Loreley
Ave Maria, by Schubert
Serenade, by Schubert
The Wanderer, by Schubert

Number 27 is a song by Baumhauer entitled "Old Donald Grey," the words by "Percival."[22] Within the large capital "O" on the title-page is tucked away a crude drawing of a three-story house surrounded by a fence, the whole engraved by G. H. Bigelow. A splendid portrait of William J. Florence,[23] lithographed by Alexander McLean of St. Louis, graces the title-page of his song "Ridin' in a Rail Road Keer" (Fig. 12).[24] A war song "Young Eph's Lamentation: Wahr Will I Go if de War Breaks de Country Up?" contrived by J. H. Murphy was copyrighted in 1862.[25] "The Sunshine of the Heart" by Filippo Pasarelli was issued in the same year.[26] "La Perle du nord," a "Mazurka élégante" by Joseph Ascher, carries no copyright claim.[27]

------

22. Copy in GML; title-page + 5 plates, copyrighted 1860.

23. See T. A. Brown, *History of the American Stage* (New York, 1870), 126.

24. Copy in GML; title-page + 4 plates numbered 29.

25. Copy in GML; title-page + 3 plates numbered 39.

26. Copy in GML; title-page + 5 plates numbered 57.

27. Copy in GML; title-page + 7 plates numbered 85.

Fig. 12. W. J. Florence, Ridin' in a Rail Road Keer (St. Louis: Jacob Endres, 1859), title-page

Neither does "Moonlight Waltz" of Franz Abt,[28] of which the collective title-page, "Jacob Endres' Edition des Danses nouvelles pour le piano," lists:

Twilight
White Rose Schottisch
Soupirs des fleurs
Gipsy Polka
Continental Polka
Camille Polka
Remember Me
Varsovianna
Josephine Mazurka
Autumn Waltz
Pleasure Train Polka
Spring Is Coming
Spring Is Coming Waltz

Two surviving songs by Ferdinand Gumbert bear no copyright claim nor plate number. "My Own Dear Native Home"[29] is number 5 on its title-page, which also records "Who Shall Be Fairest" and "How Could I Leave Thee," two songs not previously recorded. The other Gumbert song, "What in My Heart So Deep Unspoken,"[30] lists the additional title "Oh! as Fair as Poets Dreaming" from *Lucrezia Borgia.*

Richard J. Compton seems to have published sheet music separately regardless of his affiliations. He seems also to have listed all of his publications in the same plate number list. It could be inferred that he engraved his own music, but that is contradicted by the fact that many plates were engraved by A. Kane, and numerous title-pages were either engraved by N. Valtsin or lithographed by Alexander McLean. He probably did not have the tools required for music engraving. Comparatively little music has survived. Plate number 6 was assigned to the *Études de la velocité,* opus 299, book 2, by Carl Czerny--an eighteen-page job.[31] He also undoubtedly published book 1, for the pagination indicates the previous publication of twenty-three plates. Plate number 297 is carried by the Stephen Glover duet "What Are the Wild Waves Saying?"[32] The surviving copy bears the imprint of Compton & Doan. Its collective title-page, "A Collection of Standard Vocal Duets by Various Authors," yields additional titles to the ones already mentioned.

The "Sonata Pathétique," opus 13, by Beethoven was numbered 301-17.[33] This was an ambitious offering, numbering seventeen plates, but it undoubtedly sold well and was reprinted many times. The partnership of Endres and Compton is recorded in the City Directory of 1865, with headquarters at 52 North Fourth Street. The only surviving publication is "Lily of the Valley Waltz" by T. M. Brown.[34] The amalgamation of the Endres and Compton catalogs is

28. Copy in GML; title-page + 2 plates numbered 99.

29. Copy in GML; title-page + 4 plates.

30. Copy in GML; title-page + 3 plates.

31. Copy in GML.

32. Copy in GML; title-page + 5 plates; no copyright.

33. Copy in GML; title-page, but not copyrighted.

34. Imperfect copy in GML; title-page only; should have 6 plates numbered 332.

indicated by the entries on the title-page of "Far o'er the Stars Is Rest" by Franz Abt.[35] Compton either bought or borrowed the plates of this song from G. André's plate number 1125. From the collective title-page that Compton had Valtsin engrave for his edition we can cull these additional titles from his "Collection of Admired German Songs": "Stay with Me" by Abt, "Winged Messengers" by Fesca,[36] "Maid of Judah" by Kuecken, "Love's Request" and "Thou Art So Near and Yet So Far" by Reichardt, "Praise of Tears" by Schubert, "How Fair Art Thou" by Weidt, and "The Tear" by Heiser, to add to those already noted.

Compton's first surviving dated piece is "Idle Wild Mazurka" by T. M. Brown, his opus 63 and copyrighted in 1866.[37] Its very attractive title pictures a mountain scene with a lake that was lithographed by Alexander McLean. Another 1866 copyright is "Don't Refuse Galop" by Albert Mahler with a title-page engraved by N. Valtsin.[38] "The Celebrated Wildfang Galop" by Carl Faust, his opus 119, was not copyrighted.[39] "Take Care Galop" by Albert Mahler seems to be the only evidence available of the partnership of Compton & Walter, who copyrighted this piece in 1866.[40] They were located at 205 North Fourth Street. The curious design composing the title-page was engraved by Valtsin. In 1867, Compton individually copyrighted "Pas de Demons,"[41] by W. D. C. Böteführ from the music of the burlesque show *The Black Crook* (Fig. 13). The brilliantly colored title-page betrays the publisher's interest in lithography. "La Petite Fadette"[42] by Th. Bradsky was arranged by A. Willhartitz for the left hand alone. "Musical Grimaces: Fool's Gallop [*sic*]" was concocted by Karl Merz (Fig. 14).[43] The grotesque title-page was engraved by Valtsin. Both pieces were copyrighted by Compton & Doan in 1867.

The partnership of Richard J. Compton and Thomas C. Doan was first recorded in the City Directory for 1868, with headquarters at 205 North Fourth Street. The first surviving piece of Compton & Doan was copyrighted in 1867. "Skating Beauty," a mazurka by R. Frank Cardella, sported a brilliantly colored title-page lithographed by McLean (Fig. 15).[44] The remaining surviving publications were all copyrighted in 1868. Number 468 is the piano piece "L'Amore Timido, or Timid Love" by Henry Robyn.[45] "Le Rossignol," a "Morceau de Salon

---

35. Copy in GML; title-page + 4 plates (numbered 1125—André's numbering).

36. [Alexander Ernst Fesca? The composer, but not this title, is in Keck's dissertation. —Ed.]

37. Copy in GML; lithographed title-page + 4 plates numbered 378.

38. Copy in GML; engraved title-page + 3 plates numbered 412 and engraved by A. Kane.

39. Copy in GML; engraved title-page + 4 plates numbered 416, engraved by A. Kane.

40. Copy in GML; engraved title-page + 4 plates, engraved by A. Kane and numbered 422.

41. Copy in GML; lithographed title-page + 5 plates numbered 438. [Another work copyrighted by Compton in 1867 with engraved title-page + 2 plates numbered 440 is "She's Lovely as a Rose," music by Eddy Fox, arranged by Frank Cardella. Information supplied by James R. Heintze.]

42. Copy in GML; engraved title-page + 6 plates numbered 441.

43. Copy in GML; engraved title-page + 4 plates numbered 451.

44. Copy in GML; lithographed title-page + 5 plates numbered 467.

45. Copy in MHS; title-page + 7 plates.

Fig. 13. W. D. C. Bötefühl, Pas de Demons [from] *Black Crook* (St. Louis: R. J. Compton, 1867), title-page

Fig. 14. Karl Merz, Musical Grimaces: Fool's Gallop (St. Louis: Compton & Doan, 1867), title-page

pour Piano composée et arrangée par Benj. Owen," was also "Dédié avec Respect à Mons. Isidor Bush par son Protégé A. Kane."[46] "Skating Rink Waltz" as arranged by A. F. Herwig runs to four plates numbered 477.[47] A song by Jessie Williams, "Star of Home," to words by C. Vincent, has four plates numbered 480.[48] "Now What Say You Polka"[49] was transcribed by Adolf Willhartitz from Suppé's operetta *Zehn Mädchen und kein Mann*. A pupil of the Ursuline Academy put forth "Sounds from the Pines (Salut à Greenbay)," of which the elaborate title-page was engraved by Valtsin.[50] The same engraver was responsible for the very striking design of the title-page of the song by Tito Mattei "Non è ver," the Italian text of which was translated by John M. Butler.[51] A typeset song lacking a plate number was copyrighted by Compton & Doan in 1868 while they were still located at 205 North Fourth Street. "One by One the Loved Are Fading" was composed by R. Frank Cardella to the words of John Morrison and carried on its title-page a very touching deathbed scene lithographed by Alexander McLean.[52]

The removal of Compton & Doan from 205 North Fourth Street to 204 North Fifth Street was celebrated by the "Fifth Street Quick Step," written for the occasion by R. Frank Cardella (see Fig. 1, p. 2).[53] The thematic material of this lively piece consists most appropriately of the melodies "Oh Come Away" and "How Can I Leave Thee." The tunes are notated on the title-page, and the motto "Compton's Removed" is printed over the staves. The colored lithograph of the new store is placed within an oval frame, and is of historic interest. At the northeast corner of Fifth and Pine stands the three-story building that houses the factory and store of the confectioner L. Pezolt. Next door is the large four-story structure that affords abundant display space for the Estey organs and Chickering and Emerson pianos on sale, with room left on the ground floor for the spacious music store of Compton & Doan. At the curb stands an attractive carriage with two horses, and on the track in the middle of Fifth Street a streetcar drawn by horses dashes to its southern destination.

The trademark of the St. Louis Book and News Company consisted of a postage-stamp design that bore a figure with outstretched arms in the center with the word "Prodigious" under the figure; above, the address 207 Fourth Street. A running border of thirty-four of these stamps frames the title of "Prodigious Polka" by A. Hoffmann.[54] In the center of the title-page stands the same figure with outstretched hands against a background of book-filled shelves. An entirely new theme is apparent in "Blissful Moments Waltz" by the well-known composer George Schleiffarth, his opus 25, as played by the Germania Club Orchestra.[55] The title-page is embellished with a charming sketch of a youthful couple in fond embrace with flowers at their feet and doves over their heads.

---

46. Copy in GML; engraved title-page + 7 plates numbered 471.

47. Copy in MHS.

48. Copy in MHS.

49. Copy in GML; engraved title-page + 4 plates numbered 494.

50. Copy in GML; engraved title-page + 7 plates numbered 505.

51. Copy in GML; engraved title-page + 6 plates numbered 524.

52. Copy in GML; lithographed title-page + 4 plates.

53. Copy in GML; title-page + 3 plates numbered 537.

54. Copy in GML; engraved title-page + 3 plates numbered 549.

55. Copy in GML; title-page lithographed by R. P. Studley & Co. + 7 plates numbered 561.

Fig. 15. R. Frank Cardella, Skating Beauty (St. Louis: Compton & Doan, 1867), title-page

14

THE BOLLMAN CLAN

Henry Bollman was born in Magdeburg, Prussia, in 1822. As a child, he was unusually precocious and sang with his mother continuously. He eventually entered the local music school and soon mastered all of the instruments. He excelled on the piano, the violin, the contrabass, and the trombone. At the conclusion of his studies he was appointed Second Kapellmeister of the Prussian Military Band at Magdeburg. Along with innumerable *Landsleute*, he emigrated to the U.S. in the 1840s and finally settled in St. Louis in 1847. The next year he married Marie de Werthen.

During the Civil War, Bollman was engaged by the Jesuits to teach in Cincinnati, at Bardstown and St. Joseph's Academy in Kentucky, and presumably at St. Xavier's College in Ohio. However, by 1864 he was back in St. Louis again. In 1867, he entered into partnership with Jules Schatzman the music engraver, and formed the publishing concern Bollman & Schatzman. In the same year he composed and published his piano piece "Les Cloches du Couvent" (Fig. 16), which became a terrific hit and is still in use.[1]

Relatively few Bollman & Schatzman copyrights have survived. Besides "Convent Bells," the only 1867 imprints are "Violet Waltz" by M. Pollatscheck, numbered 120, and "Falling Leaves Mazurka" by G. Winter and numbered 160. Then there is an 1872 copyright, the song with chorus "Birdie Darling," the words by V. J. Engle, the music by Henry Bollman, the plate number 801. There are some reprints that were not copyrighted: number 101, "Ah! So Pure" from Auber's *Martha*; 136, "Alpine Bells" by Theodore Oesten; 411, "Loreley," and 414, "Switzer's Farewell," both transcribed by Daniel Krug; 827, the song "Juanita" transcribed by Brinley Richards; and "Tyrolien Melody" by Krug but printed from the plates of G. André & Company and possibly bearing their plate number 807.[2]

The extent of the Bollman & Schatzman catalog may be gauged by studying the collective title-pages on the pieces enumerated so far. The title-page of "Violet Waltz" lists:

> "Recreation Schottisch," by Beyer
> "Woodland Home Waltz," by Bierman
> "Ambrosia Schottisch," by Bierman
> "Bright Hours Polka," by Brunner
> "Welcome Home Schottisch," by Brunner
> "Willie's Favorite Waltz," by Brunner
> "Fairy Dell March," by Conner
> "Olympic Waltz," by Ford
> "Remember Me Polka," by Koenig
> "Gipsy March," by Morris
> "Delicioso Waltz," by Needham
> "Merry Time Galop," by Needham

---

1. [Copy at GML.]

2. [George Keck's correction from Krohn's typescript--plate number 887. Copies of all publications cited in this paragraph are at the GML.]

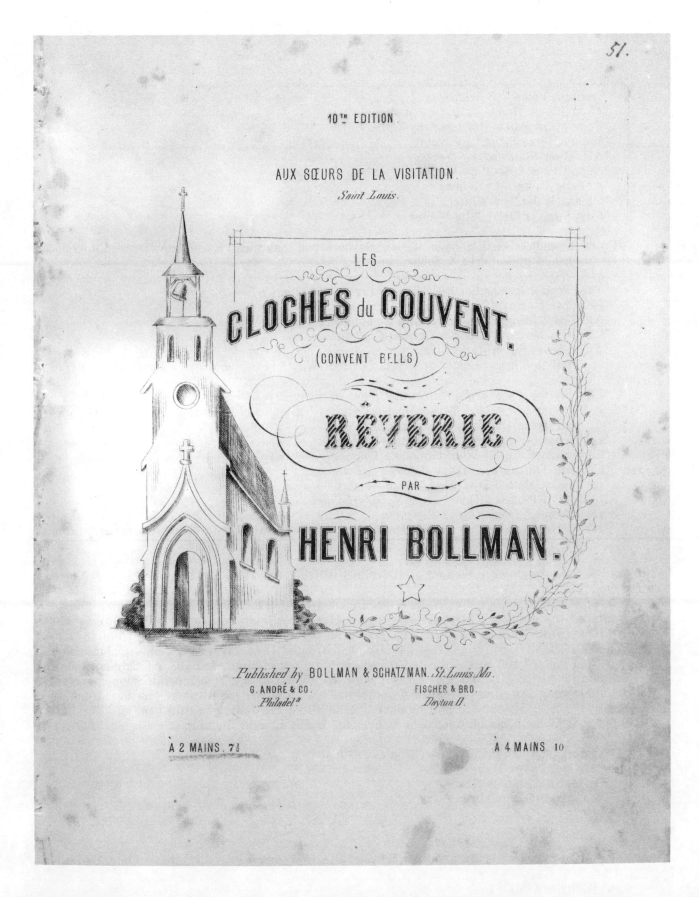

Fig. 16. Henri Bollman, Les Cloches du Couvent (Convent Bells): Reverie (St. Louis: Bollman & Schatzman, 1867), title-page

> "Daisy Waltz," by Pollatscheck
> "Starlight Polka," by Richards
> "Thoughts of Home Waltz," by Southfield
> "Rosy Morn Polka Mazurka," by Waller[3]
> "Happy Home Polka," by Weber
> "Affection Redowa," by Werner
> "Happy Face Polka," by Winter
> "Annette Galop," by Winter
> "Vienna Waltz," by Winter
> "First Success Galop," by Winter

From the collective title-page of "Ah! So Pure" we may glean a number of operatic compositions published by Bollman & Schatzman:

> "Then You'll Remember Me," from Balfe's *Bohemian Girl*
> "Hear Me Norma," from Bellini's *Norma*
> "Ah! Don't Mingle," from Bellini's *Sonnambula*
> "Life Has No Power," from Donizetti's *Belisario*
> "Angel So Pure," from Donizetti's *La Favorita*
> "All Hail to Thee, France" and "Ask Me Not Why," from Donizetti's *La Fille du Régiment*
> "I'll Pray for Thee" from Donizetti's *Lucia di Lammermoor*
> "It Is Better to Laugh," "Make Me No Gaudy Chaplet," and "Oh! as Fair as Poets Dreaming," from Donizetti's *Lucrezia Borgia*
> "Last Rose of Summer," from Flotow's *Martha*
> "Language of Love," from Gounod's *Faust*
> "Call Me Thine Own," from Halévy's *L'Éclair*
> "In These Celestial Dwellings," from Mozart's *Magic Flute*
> "In Tears I Pine for Thee," from Verdi's *Lombardi*
> "Dear Name," from Verdi's *Rigoletto*
> "Ah! I Have Sighed to Rest," "Home to Our Mountains," and "Rosy Morning," from Verdi's *Il Trovatore*

Bollman & Schatzman were located at 107 North Fifth from 1867 to 1869, and at 111 North Fifth from 1870 to 1873.

In 1874, Schatzman seems to have severed his partnership with Henry Bollman and to have entered the employ of Balmer & Weber. Henry Bollman continued publishing at 111 North Fifth. From 1876 to 1879 he was located on Olive Street, first at 609 and from 1877 to 1879 at 619. The only copyright that has survived is dated 1874. It was Bollman's composition entitled "Ilda Waltz," and was dedicated to Ilda Mathey. It is numbered 1035.[4] Bollman seems to have continued the plate number series begun with Schatzman. Two reprints have survived: the Schubert song "The Last Greeting," numbered 532, and the piano piece "La Baladine" by Charles B. Lysberg, his opus 51 and numbered 818. From the collective title-page of "The Last Greeting" it is evident that he published many songs by Franz Abt, including:

> Agathe, or When the Swallows Homeward Fly
> All Alone, Ever There
> Far o'er the Stars Is Rest
> Goodnight! Goodnight!

---

3. [Sidney Waller? This composer, but not this title, given in Keck's dissertation. —Ed.]

4. [Copy at GML.]

Herdsman's Mountain Home
Irene, or Whether I Love Thee
It Was Not Thus to Be
Kathleen Aroon
Native Home
In the Eye There Lies the Heart
O Ye Tears
Sleep Well, Thou Sweet Angel
Springtime
Stay with Me
Thoughts of Home

From the same title-page we can gather other vocal publications:

"Ah! Could I Teach the Nightingale," by Keller
"Adelaide," by Beethoven
"My Home," by Doppler
"The Tear" and "What in My Heart So Deep Unspoken," by Gumbert
"Through Meadows Green," by Haas
"Ah! Gentle Eye," by Heiser
"Drift My Bark," "Friendly Is Thine Air," "Gently Rest," "Good Night Farewell," "The
      Hunters," and "Weep Not Fond Heart," by Kuecken
"We'll Meet Above," by Liebe
"Come Lovely May" and "In These Celestial Dwellings," by Mozart
"Greeting," by Mendelssohn
"Alpine Horn" and "Youth by the Brook," by Proch
"Image of the Rose" and "Thou Art So Near and Yet So Far," by Reichardt
"The Red Sarafan," Russian song
"Serenade" and "The Wanderer," by Schubert
"How Can I Leave Thee," by Abt
"The Brightest Eyes" and "Tyrolese and His Child," by Stigelli[5]
"How Fair Art Thou," by Weidt
"Serenade to Ida," by Weingand

Henry Bollman also published Czerny's *School of Velocity* and *100 Easy and Progressive Exercises*, Diabelli's *28 Melodious Exercises*, Duvernoy's *École du mecanisme*, and Köhler's *First Studies*, op. 50. From the title-page of Lysberg's "La Baladine" many more piano pieces emerge, including:

"Belle de nuit," "Cascade des roses," and "Mazurka des trainaux," by Ascher
"Maiden's Prayer," by Badarzewska
"Herzweh," by Behr
"Les Bords du Missouri," "Orpheus Grand Waltz," and "La Tendresse Grand Waltz," by
      Bollman
"Il Desiderio" and "Last Idea of Weber," by Cramer
"Aubade," by Dorn
"Dream on the Ocean," by Gungl
"Remember Me," by August Held
"Qui Vive Galop," by Ganz
"Heimweh," by Jungmann
"Argentine Mazurka" "Bout-en-train Galop," "Caprice hongroise," "Caprice militaire,"
      "Galop di bravoura," "Gaetana Mazurka," and "Grand Galop de concert," by Ketterer

---

5. [Presumably Giorgio Stigelli. —Ed.]

"Lauterbach Maiden," by Loffler[6]
"Alpine Bells," "Alpine Songs," "Carnaval de Venise," "Ernani Fantasie," "Gondellied,"
      "Home Sweet Home," "La Melancolie," "Love in May," "Thou Art So Near and Yet
      So Far," and "When the Swallows Homeward Fly," by Oesten
"La Pluie des perles Waltz," by Osborne
"Echo of Lucerne" and "Her Bright Smile Haunts Me," by Richards
"Floating on the Wine," "Juanita," "Warblings at Eve," "What Are the Wild Waves Saying,"
      by Richards
"Home Sweet Home," variations by Slack
"Harpe aeolienne" and "Lily of the Valley," by Sidney Smith
"On the Beautiful Blue Danube," by Strauss
"Then You'll Remember Me," by Voss[7]
"Monastery Bells," by Wely
"Il Bacio," by Werner

   In 1880, Henry Bollman brought his sons Otto, Oscar, and Norman into the business,
using the name Henry Bollman & Sons. From 1880 to 1884 the firm was located at 206 North
Fifth Street. During 1883 and 1884 the address changed to 208-10 North Broadway. From
1885 to 1890, the firm held forth on Olive Street, at first at 1104-06 and then at 1100. The
only dated copyright that has survived is the song "You," by A. G. Robyn. The edition in the
key of C was published in 1884, and that in B-flat was issued in 1891. The soprano edition is
not available.
   Several reprints have survived, including Sonatina, op. 36, no. 2, by Clementi and numbered 789; "Faust Fantaisie Élégante" by Leybach, numbered 1037; the song "We'll Meet Above"
by Louis Liebe, numbered 1123; the piano piece "Fantasie sur un thème allemande" by Leybach,
his opus 5, numbered 1766; the song "I Cannot Say Goodbye" by Joseph L. Roeckel, number
773; "Love's Proving," by Frederick N. Loehr, number 2531; "Lucia Fantasie" by Joseph Ascher,
his opus 27 and numbered 2538.
   Many more titles may be gleaned from collective title-pages. From "Faust Fantaisie
Élégante," there are other Leybach pieces, including:

Première Nocturne, op. 3
Deuxième Nocturne, op. 4
Fantasie on Puritani, op. 48
Cinquième Nocturne, op. 52
Tyrolienne, op. 54
Chant du Proscrit, op. 75
Freischuetz Fantasie, op. 96
Première Grand Valse brillante, op. 14
Deuxième Valse brillante, op. 20
Norma Fantaisie brillante, op. 65
Sonnambula Fantasie, op. 27
Septième Nocturne, op. 111

---

   6. [Krohn's typescript spells the composer "Loeffler"; "Loffler," with this title, comes
from Keck's dissertation. —Ed.]

   7. [Presumably Charles Voss, which composer (but not this title) is included in Keck's
dissertation. —Ed.]

From Leybach's "Fantasie sur un thème allemande" others may be gathered, including:

"L'Éclair Nocturne" and "Fanfara militaire," by Ascher
"Silent Thoughts," by Bohm
"Lucia di Lammermoor," "Il Trovatore," and "Martha," by Dorn
"Nocturne," by Döhler
"Mocking Bird," by Grobe
"The Mill," by Kuhe
"Enticement Waltz," "Hortensia," "Fond Hearts Must Part," and "Thine Own," by Lange
"Pearly Cascade," by Lichner[8]
"Kathleen Mavourneen," by Brinley Richards
"La Cascade de Rubis," by Sidney Smith
"Charge of the Hussars," by Spindler[9]
"Titania Fantasie de concert," by Wely
"Album Leaf," by Kirchner

We could add some Eugene Ketterer items, including "Vienne Galop," "Valse des fleurs," and "Defile March."
From the collective title-page of "The Youth by the Brook" come some additional titles:

"Ah! Gentle Eye," by Heiser
"Adieu to the Woodlands," "Dame Swallow Soars Aloft," "Goodnight My Child," "Perplexity," "The Rose and the Nightingale," "Tyrolese and His Child," and "Wanderer's Dream," by Franz Abt
"Then You'll Remember Me," by Balfe
"Home Sweet Home," by Bishop
"Long Weary Day," German folksong
"If on the Meads I Cast My View," "Sad Is My Heart with Care," "Ye Merry Birds," by Gumbert
"The Tear," by Heiser
"Two Nightingales," by Hackel
"May Breezes," by Kreipl
"Ah! Could I Teach the Nightingale," by Keller
"Oh! Come to Me," "Oh! Thou Art Like a Flower," "Oh! Wert Thou but My Own Love," "Swallow's Farewell," and "We Met by Chance," by Kuecken
"Where Roses Fair," by Gustav
"Must I Then Part from Thee," by Liebe
"I Would That My Love" and "Oh! Wert Thou in the Cold Blast," by Mendelssohn
"Gipsy Boy in the North," by Reissiger[10]
"Thou Art So Near and Yet So Far," by Reichardt
"Last Greeting," by Schubert
"Last Rose of Summer," by Flotow
"Spring and Love," by Siebert
"Broken Ring," folksong
"When the Quiet Moon Is Beaming," by Schorndorf

---

8. [Heinrich Lichner? This composer, but not this title, is in Keck's dissertation. —Ed.]

9. [Fritz Spindler? This composer, but not this title, is listed in Keck's dissertation. —Ed.]

10. [Carl Gottlieb Reissiger? This composer, but not this title, listed in Keck's dissertation. —Ed.]

"Three Students," by Speyer
"Her Bright Smile Haunts Me Still," by W. T. Wrighton

Several more titles may be gleaned from the title-page of Loehr's song "Love's Proving," notably:

"Thee Only I Love," by Abt
"Alice Where Art Thou," by Ascher
"Again I Hear My Mother Sing," by Carl Bohm
"Her King," by Blumenthal
"You Think I Have a Merry Heart," by Brunner
"The Sunny Month of May," by Beatrice
"The Angel Came," by Cowen
"Together" and "Star of My Heart," by Denza
"Open Thy Lattice," by L. Gregh
"Darling Mine, Forget Me Not," by H. Ford
"Last Night," by Kjerulf
"Dear Heart," by Mattei
"A Leaf from the Spray," by Mey
"Best of All," by Moir
"Love's Old Sweet Song" and "Oh! How Delightful," by Molloy
"Calvary," by Rodney
"Bid Me Goodbye," by Tosti[11]
"Song of My Heart," by Watson
"Little Fishermaiden," by Waldmann

Henry Bollman died on 25 December 1890. The firm was reorganized as Bollman Brothers Music Company with the store at 1100 Olive Street. This was changed to 1120 Olive Street in 1903 and remained there through 1913. Only three publications seem to have survived, all by Carl Wilhelm Kern: "Sweet Forget Me Not Polka," opus 1 (1893), the song "Spring Day," opus 16 (1893), and "El Parado, Gavotte Mexicana," opus 20 (1892). They also published Kern's opus 2, "Blue Violet Polka"; opus 4, "Always Gay Mazurka"; opus 6, "Picnic Gavotte"; opus 7, "Flower Polka"; opus 9, "Dawn of the Day March"; and opus 17, "The Cavalier."

Bollman Brothers Music Company seems to have ceased publishing around 1900 and became an organization concentrating on the sale of pianos. The store at 1120 Olive Street was unusually large and was completely filled with pianos.

------

11. [The title given as "Good-bye," by F. Paolo Tosti, in another edition (Baltimore: G. Willig, [1868-1910]) listed in Keck's dissertation. —Ed.]

15

THE AMAZING KUNKELS

From the Rheinpfalz in Germany emerged two youngsters who were destined to become outstanding pianists: Carl Kunkel, born in 1840, and Jacob, born in 1846. Following the trend of many German families of this period, their folks emigrated to the U.S., and in 1848 reached Cincinnati where the boys spent their youth. The elder Kunkel instructed them in piano playing so that as they matured they were well grounded in their art. Carl was the aggressive one who not only gave piano recitals, going so far afield as New York City, but also became associated with Louis Moreau Gottschalk doing two-piano work in concert tours. In 1868, the brothers moved to St. Louis with their families and established a music store. In 1872, they founded the St. Louis Conservatory of Music, and in 1878 began the publication of *Kunkel's Musical Review*, which acted as a propaganda sheet for their publications. The *Musical Review* was long-lived, and lasted until the early twentieth century. The *Review* had a group of notable editors who at times managed to produce brilliant editions. The first editor was H. Gordon Temple, who functioned to 1 March 1880. He was succeeded by Irenaeus D. Foulon, A.B., L.L.B., lawyer and musical amateur, who seems to have been active until 1888. He proved to be a very capable editor. In 1889, Thomas Hyland took over and apparently acted as editor until the journal gradually expired in 1904. The exact date of the last issue is unknown. The only tolerably complete file was bound up by Tom Hyland, but it lacks the last issues. Sooner or later they will turn up.

The *Review* contains priceless notes on music in St. Louis as well as informative articles by local musicians. It also contains very interesting advertisements inserted by local schools and individual teachers. It really was the advertising matter that kept it alive for such a long time.

Although both brothers had done some publishing in Cincinnati, it was a drop in the bucket compared to what they did in St. Louis. It is not known when they published their first piece, although they did print two guitar pieces by William O. Bateman in 1876. Jacob was the most talented of the two, but he died in 1882 and did not have enough time to develop his talent. He did write some brilliant piano pieces that he sold to Julie Rivé-King, who wished to appear on her innumerable piano solo programs as a composer. Outstanding among these is "On Blooming Meadows," which became tremendously popular.

Carl, now known as Charles, compiled a *Royal Piano Method* that ran to several volumes and became an exceedingly popular elementary method. He issued all of the standard works of a technical nature, such as those by Bertini, Burgmüller, Clementi, Cramer, Czerny, Duvernoy, Loeschhorn, which were usually edited by "Hans von Buelow," "Carl Tausig," or any other pianists who happened to strike his fancy. Needless to say, none of these editors ever saw the proof-sheets of the works that they were purported to have edited.

While Charles Kunkel had very little talent for composition, he was an excellent editor. He edited everything, not hesitating to change anything that he thought needed improving. He had an excellent engraver, Phillip Steiner, who was kept busy on a full-time basis engraving all of Kunkel's fabrications. When compositions did not look like they would hit the best-seller list, he printed them on the copper-plate press in runs as low as twenty-five copies. His masterpiece was "Alpine Storm" (Fig. 17), which was a big seller. It was an outright steal from "Storm" by Henry Weber, which in turn was an adaptation of the storm movement in Beethoven's "Pastoral" Symphony. Kunkel dished out so many easy teaching pieces that he had recourse to many pseudonyms. The most useful ones were Claude Melnotte, Jean Paul, Carl

Fig. 17. Charles Kunkel, Alpine Storm (St. Louis: Kunkel Bros., 1888), title-page

Sidus,[12] and the names of numerous students and female favorites. Although Kunkel copyrighted everything he published, he paid precious little attention to the copyrights on other music. He was unscrupulous and stole right and left.

The brightest aspect of his work was the encouragement that he gave to local composers. He published all of the early piano pieces of Ernest R. Kroeger, from opus 1 to 28. Other local composers whose pieces he published were Otto Anschuetz, William D. Armstrong (of Alton), Emile and Lucien Becker, John W. Boone, Louis Conrath, Marcus and A. I. Epstein, I. D. Foulon, Robert Goldbeck, August William Hoffman, J. A. Kieselhorst, Nicholas Lebrun, J. F. and Albert Mahler, Paul Mori, Richard S. Poppen, Louis Retter, John J. Voellmecke, August Waldauer, and many others. To be sure, many of these fell into the "twenty-five copies" category. Others were Herman Epstein, Waldemar Malmene, Alfred G. Robyn, Regina M. Carlin, Fleta Jan Brown, William Theodore Diebels, William Schuyler, McNair Ilgenfritz, Ottmar Moll, Charles Galloway, Arnold Pesold, Carl Wilhelm Kern, and so on.

As an editor, Kunkel frequently over-edited his pieces, providing as many as three sets of fingerings for difficult passages. Conspicuous were the arrows that indicated which phrases were to be played from the wrist. He was at his best in indicating the pedaling. Nothing was left to chance. He published a *Kunkel's Pedal Method* which was really a steal from Köhler. He published many pieces with pedal notations--notes and rests--to indicate the exact duration of the depression of the right pedal. He also published many pieces with the pedaling indicated by lines. This was perhaps the best and the most useful. Later in his career, he used the usual pedaling signs--"Ped." and an asterisk--but was very careful about their placement. The use of curved lines over notes has always plagued pianists, for the curved lines may indicate the grammatical content of the music, or they may indicate the manner in which it is to be played--in other words, the articulation or the phrasing. Books have been written on these subjects, and still editors and composers do not realize the importance of keeping them separated. Kunkel did not have any radical ideas about either subject, but he managed to keep his text so marked that it could be easily comprehended. In a general way he edited his publications in a manner far superior to that practiced by all of the well-known eastern publishers. The only competition was furnished by Shattinger, who had a magnificent editor in the person of Carl Wilhelm Kern.

In his earlier publications Kunkel paid attention to his title-pages. In fact, he had many colored lithographed pages. Such a one was the billiard table which was outstanding in its design. The faces were all authentic. He had also many black and white pages such as the excellent "Union Pacific Railroad March," which was very effectively designed. He made much use of collective title-pages. He would also design a one-composer title-page with room for all of that composer's pieces he published.

Charles Kunkel was an excellent sight-reader. He and his brother Jacob excelled in two-piano playing. That is what brought him to the attention of Louis Moreau Gottschalk. When he toured as part of the Gottschalk concert troupe, he and Gottschalk usually played two-piano pieces on their many concert appearances. After his brother's death he usually did two-piano work with some visiting pianist. Moritz Rosenthal particularly enjoyed playing with him.

My first introduction to Kunkel occurred at his store in a residence on Locust Street. The music counter was in the rear of the building. To the front were several parlors and a grand staircase. I was waiting for the girl to fill my order. Suddenly a terrible commotion seemed to be transpiring upstairs. The noise was drifting downstairs. It seems that Kunkel's sons were trying to keep him from coming downstairs. He owerpowered them and gained the main floor. In his rage he picked up a convenient glass inkwell and hurled it through the glass French door. After this catastrophe all was quiet. And what was this all about? It appears that one of the girls had hung a picture the wrong way, and he was going to "get" that girl. Needless to say, the girl ran out of the building as soon as the racket started. I had to run after her to bring her the jacket she left on the counter. This was a mild demonstration of his ungovernable temper.

The amazing thing about Kunkel was the vast contrast between his career as a music publisher and his actual personality. In his younger days he must have been a very refined young

---

12. [See, e.g., Sidus's "Christmas Bells," op. 214 (!), 1890. —James R. Heintze.]

man. His concert appearances as a soloist gave promise of a tremendous potentiality as a concert artist. In his St. Louis days he developed a striking personality, but one that was more remarkable for its vulgarity than for its artistic maturity. (For years, Charles Van Ravenswaay wanted me to write a biographical sketch of Kunkel for publication in the *Bulletin of the Missouri Historical Society*. I could never see my way to doing it for the simple reason that the usual stories that one tells about one's hero would have been too vulgar to print.)

It happened that he reprinted one of the well-known waltzes of Moritz Moszkowski. When his print reached Europe, Moszkowski became so incensed that he threatened to take the next ship over and shoot the perpetrator. Moszkowski had ample justification for his emotional excitement over Kunkel's treatment of his piano piece. The composition in question was originally published by Julius Hainauer of Breslau as one of a group of "Trois Morceaux," oeuvre 34, no. 1, "Valse in E major." It contained seventeen plates and the text was amply spaced. Kunkel crowded the seventeen plates into eleven, usually by omitting some of Moszkowski's music. He cut down the introduction from fifty-two to eighteen measures of his own invention. The only portions that he left untouched were the main and secondary themes, although he rearranged the accompaniment. In fact, although he freely altered all intervening sections, he left the right hand part of the main themes intact. To cap the climax, he wrote an entirely new finale and completely discarded the original coda. Shooting would have been painless; he should have been hanged at sunrise. If all of his reprints were similarly manhandled, they must have been worthless as teaching material. Yet they sold well. Most teachers did not go to the trouble of checking his reprints with the European originals.

16

THE ENTERPRISING SHATTINGERS

Some time in the 1840s, Thomas Shattinger left his native Bavaria and went to New Orleans to seek his fortune in the New World. Being a ship-builder, he had no difficulty in finding employment, for this was the era of riverboats on the Mississippi. As soon as he was settled, he sent for his wife Barbara and the four children. Tragically, they reached New Orleans only to find that Thomas had died of yellow fever a few weeks before their arrival. Barbara fended for her brood as well as she could and eventually moved to Cincinnati. Here, her eldest son Adam got into the saddlery business. In due course of time his guitar playing brought him to the attention of Jacob Kunkel, the pianist. Kunkel wanted him to learn the music engraving business so that he could be helpful in the Kunkel publishing program. Unfortunately, Adam had but one good eye. His eye doctor thought that music engraving would be too much of a strain on that eye and advised against it. Through his guitar playing he became intimate with the Kunkel family, and in 1865 he married Mary, the sister of Jacob Kunkel. When the Kunkels moved to St. Louis he followed them and became a clerk in their music store. His interest in music centered on the guitar, for he had acquired a mastery of that instrument.

In 1876, Shattinger left the Kunkel establishment to found his own music store. It was located at 16 South Fifth Street, but in 1879 it was moved to 19 South Fifth. Shattinger was located at 1114 Olive Street from 1897 to 1900, at 912 Olive Street from 1904 to 1920, at 1103 Olive Street from 1921 to 1923. A disastrous fire that originated in an adjoining store gutted the Shattinger premises and completely ruined the stock of sheet music in 1923. A new store was immediately opened up in the Arcade Building at 812 Olive Street. Several large rooms were converted into a music store and a room across the hall was used as a piano display room.

To return to the story of Adam Shattinger and the formation of his music publishing business, those were the days of B. F. Shaw & Company of Philadelphia, who reprinted innumerable pieces of music, always leaving a large space on the collective title-page for a new publisher's name. Many of Adam Shattinger's early publications were of this type. Adam Shattinger published his first piece, "The Cuckoo" by Lutz, in 1872. This piece carries the plate number 1. The next surviving piece, number 52, is "Convent Bells" by Spindler,[1] and number 55 is "Idylle" by Charles B. Lysberg These were not copyrighted. Another 1872 issue was "Spring Flower Mazurka" by Millie Sherman, numbered 96. Several 1874 copyrights have survived. "Happy Greeting Schottische" is numbered 127, "Lauterbach Waltz" by Lutz 136, and "Irresistible Schottische" by William Siebert is numbered 139. Copyrights of 1875 include "Carols of Birds," numbered 145, and "Chanson d'amour," numbered 146, both by Siebert. In 1876 Shattinger copyrighted "High Up on the Hill" by C. Bumiller, numbered 61. "My Little Lee's March" by Eugene Le Beust, numbered 95, was copyrighted in 1878. An 1879 copyright is "Loving Eyes" by F. S. Collender, numbered 190. It was obvious that he was publishing a lot of teaching music. In this he was but following the example of Balmer & Weber.

Shattinger's greatest achievement was his publication in 1881 of William O. Bateman's *School of the Guitarist*. Bateman was a successful lawyer whose hobby was music. He not only

---

1. [Fritz Spindler? This composer, but not this title, is listed in Keck's dissertation. —Ed.]

composed guitar music but he also taught guitar playing and music engraving. Bateman's magnificent guitar method consists of numerous exercises and a number of fine transcriptions for the guitar. Many of these pieces were published separately.[2] Shattinger was a fine guitar player and always took the greatest interest in guitar music.

In 1896, Shattinger incorporated his business as the Shattinger Piano and Music Company, and in 1897 his youngest son Oliver entered the business. Oliver was born in the apartment over the store at 10 South Fifth Street on 3 September 1879. The Shattingers sold sheet music, pianos, organs, violins, and other musical instruments, in addition to publishing much piano music, mainly for teaching purposes. Over the years, Shattinger availed himself of the services of several editors, including Charles Machacheck, Otto Anschuetz, Louis Hammerstein, Victor Ehling, and Leo Miller. Ernest R. Kroeger was really editor of Thiebes & Stierlin, but he did some work for Shattinger.

In 1903, Shattinger acquired Carl Wilhelm Kern as editor. Kern was a gifted composer with a rich melodic vein. As an editor he was far superior to Charles Kunkel, being specifically more modern in his approach and possessing greater artistic integrity. Under his sponsorship the Shattinger catalog acquired a freshness and a richness that made it outstanding. The compositions of contemporary composers were published, but only if they measured up to his high standard of musicianship. The emphasis was on music for the elementary grades. Music in the fourth and fifth grades of difficulty was published but only if it was attractive, not only melodically but harmonically as well. It also had to be pedagogically practical. The Shattinger publications blossomed forth and were eagerly incorporated into the teaching repertory.

In 1907, the writer of these lines was engaged as order clerk. Having by this time acquired a fair proficiency as a pianist, I had no difficulty in adjusting myself to the problems of music editing. In fact, my experience as order clerk gave me a solid basis for my future career as a music bibliographer. Since I had to prepare covers for the never-ending flow of new music from Schirmer, Ditson, Schmidt, *et al.*, I acquired a high degree of expertness in writing the vertical script that was deemed essential for these covers. Fifty years later I became bibliographically involved at Gaylord Music Library and wrote some twenty-five thousand covers using this self-same script.

Meanwhile, in 1909, I had become encouraged to take up piano teaching. Ella Krieckhaus had all along been insisting that I should teach and not just sell music. In fact, she very sweetly told me that if she found me in the store the next week she would pick me up and toss me out on Olive Street. And she was big enough to do it. Fortunately, Adam Shattinger laid me off for three weeks that Saturday. I utilized the time by soliciting piano pupils, and was so successful that at the end of three weeks I could return to the store and hand Mr. Shattinger my card as a piano teacher. Not only that, but I actually doubled my income by taking up teaching. Shattinger was so impressed that he engaged me as assistant to Carl Wilhelm Kern, which position I held for forty years thereafter.

At the death of Adam Shattinger in 1917, Oliver took over and carried on the policy that had been so successful. Upon the dissolution of Balmer & Weber in 1909, their stock of sheet music and musical merchandise had been acquired. Eventually, the catalogs of Thiebes & Stierlin and Val Reis were absorbed by the growing Shattinger catalog. With the removal of the store to the Arcade Building, organ and choral music began to appear. Paul Friess was specifically engaged to edit this music. I was directed to prepare a graded catalog of the piano music based on the new scheme adopted by the MTNA in 1919.

The music to be published was engraved by Phillip Steiner and his son Edward. They cooperated very effectively in carrying out the editorial ideas conceived by Carl Wilhelm Kern. He had made a careful study of phrasing and articulation, and made every composition conform to his progressive ideas on these subjects. This made for greater consistency in the musical picture of the published composition. This also made it possible for the teacher to adhere to a

---

2. [Krohn originally included titles here, but they are also given above in chapter 12. —Ed.]

more plausible interpretation of his text. Since I was the better pianist of the editorial staff, I was entrusted with the fingering and pedaling. My edition of the C-sharp minor Prelude of Rachmaninoff became a classic, for I had taken notes on his use of the sostenuto pedal and incorporated his practice in my edition.

Local composers were liberally represented in the Shattinger catalog. Most of these were of the "bought and paid for" variety. Frequently the composer's compensation consisted of twenty-five copies of the printed music. Shattinger offered me twenty-five copies of my "Valse Serenade." We finally settled on fifteen dollars and twenty-five copies which I sold to my pupils for fifty cents apiece. Editorial work was vastly underpaid. That was largely the fault of Carl Wilhelm Kern, who did not insist on adequate compensation. However, since he wrote a set of ten pieces for every publisher in the U.S., he was never really financially embarrassed. His opus numbers ran over a thousand and he had in print over two thousand compositions. He wrote over a number of pseudonyms of which the usual ones were Ludwig Renk, Jean Navarre, J. Dudley Martin, Dudley Ryder, Neruda, Fr. Faerber, and Kenneth Foster. The local composers represented in the Shattinger catalog were:

Otto Anschuetz
Samuel Aronson
William O. Bateman
Samuel Bollinger
Robert Buechler
C. Bumiller
Porter Burnett
Regina Carlin
J. Cassin
Gregory Cohn
Jean Diestelhorst (her pseudonym was Jean Dale)
Harvey Enders
Marcus Epstein
M. Teresa Finn
Lucien Fordel (pseudonym of Lilie Bindbuetel)
Robert Goldbeck
Max Gottschalk
Hugo Hagen
Felix Heink
Alexander Henneman
Lydia Henniger
Daniel Jones
Elmer Keeton
Carl Wilhelm Kern
Ernest R. Kroeger
Ernst Krohn, Sr.[3]
Ernst C. Krohn
Ellis Levy
Arthur Lieber
Edwin Vaile McIntyre
Albert Mengel
Edward Menges
Robert Miller
Paul Mori
Chester Nordman

---

3. [Ernst Ludwig Krohn, the author's father. —Ed.]

Anna Mae Loewenstein Nussbaum
Nathan Sachs
Albert Scholin
William Siebert
Walter Stockhoff
Katherine Tenner
Gerald Tyler
Henry Stanley Walser
June Weybright
Richard Whiting
V. T. Williams
M. Yuill

Few composers of educational literature realize how necessary it is to keep within the confines of one grade. The conception is a vital one in music publishing. A teacher should have at his disposal a carefully graduated series of texts. For years editors and publishers have been floundering around in a vain attempt to arrive at a practical scheme of grading. The technical difficulties in piano playing may be arranged in groups usually called grades. The number of grades has ranged from six to eleven, with seven as the common denominator. I touched upon this in my chapter on Balmer & Weber. In 1918, I read a paper at the annual meeting of the Music Teachers National Association in St. Louis on "Some Fundamental Considerations in Grading Elementary Piano Music." This essay was not only published in the *Proceedings of the MTNA* for 1918 but also in the April 1919 issue of *The Musician*. At the conclusion of my paper, William Arms Fisher proposed the appointment of a commission to prepare a definite scheme of grading. The members of that commission were Fisher, William Lawrence Calhoun, and myself. We deliberated by mail and finally arrived at a classification of the specifications of each grade. This was published in a booklet and mailed to the members of the MTNA.

It will be instructive to publish a brief summary of the findings of the commission. The first grade must remain within the confines of the five-finger position. The second grade may move around a little and may use double notes in either hand. The third grade may drop to low bass notes and play simple chords. The fourth grade may use octaves and full chords in either hand and may indulge in scales and simple arpeggios. The fifth grade may use diatonic double thirds and similar intricate figuration, and may use chromatic and full chords and diminished seventh chords and arpeggios. The sixth grade may use chromatic double thirds and may indulge in greater speed. The seventh grade may use chromatic double sixths and fourths, and may resort to any type of technical difficulty.

17

THE EMERGENCE OF RAGTIME

During the last decade of the nineteenth century there emerged in the playing of countless black piano players of dance music a new rhythm. It was based primarily on the rhythms of black folk music and soon permeated all dance music, marches, and cakewalks. Eventually it acquired its own distinctive name--ragtime. The earliest publications of ragtime were compositions of Caucasian musicians. In January of 1897 William Krell, the well-known bandmaster, published his "Mississippi Rag," the first ragtime two-step ever written, and first played by Krell's Orchestra in Chicago. The themes include a cakewalk, a plantation song, and a "buck-and-wing" dance.

Since ragtime was actually a form of black folk music, its legitimate composer should have been black. The first ragtime piece by a black composer is "Harlem Rag" by Tom Turpin, published by Robert de Yong in St. Louis in December 1897.

Thomas Million (Milton) Turpin was born in the early 1870s in Savannah, Georgia. He came to St. Louis in 1880 and eventually established himself at 2200 Market Street where he was proprietor of the Rosebud Cafe. He had a bar in the front and a wine room with tables in the rear. His upright piano stood in the wine room, which soon became the rendezvous of every visiting ragtime pianist. The Hurrah Sporting Club, in a shack a block away, also had a piano. The rapid development of ragtime was due to the competitive jam sessions held in just such localities. Tom Turpin improvised innumerable rags, but only five were ever published. He died in St. Louis on 13 August 1922.

The second published black rag is "Ma Ragtime Baby," composed by Fred Stone of Detroit and published there by Whitney and Warren in 1898. The third black ragtime piece is "Original Rags" composed by Scott Joplin, published by Carl Hoffman in Kansas City in March 1899. Scott Joplin was born in Texarkana, Arkansas, on 24 November 1868. He early gave evidence of his musical gift and in the course of time started to drift here and there in pursuit of musical employment. In 1885 he came to St. Louis, where he stayed eight years. In 1893 he went to the Chicago World's Fair where he recruited a band. After the Fair he returned to St. Louis, but in 1894 transferred his operations to Sedalia, Missouri. This town had more than its share of ragtime background, and he soon began to compose. In 1897, he attended the George Smith College for Negroes and acquired a substantial theoretical background for his future work. His second ragtime piece is "Maple Leaf Rag" (Fig. 18), published by John Stark & Son in Sedalia in September 1899. The "Maple Leaf Rag" became a terrific success and made the reputations of both Joplin and Stark.

Stark transferred his business to St. Louis, and Joplin followed him there. Stark had great faith in ragtime and specialized in the production of the creations of his ragtime collaborators. So-called "legitimate publishers" would have nothing to do with this new type of music. In fact, since most of it was cradled in the gambling dens and bordellos of the larger cities, it was not quite respectable, so John Stark had the field to himself. Arrived in St. Louis, he domiciled his family and business at 3848 Washington Avenue. Eventually, the profits from "Maple Leaf Rag" enabled him to acquire a printing plant at 3615 Laclede Avenue and he soon established a profitable publishing business.

Before he left Sedalia, Joplin married Belle Hayden, a widow and sister-in-law of Scott Hayden, another redoubtable ragtime pianist. They lived at 2658 Morgan Street. Eventually Scott Hayden and his wife moved in with them. Now began a busy time for Joplin. In 1901 he

Fig. 18. Scott Joplin, Maple Leaf Rag (Sedalia, Mo.: John Stark & Son, 1899), title-page

published "Easy Winner Rag," and Stark published "Peacherino." In 1902, Stark put forth "Entertainer Rag," "Strenuous Life," "Elite Syncopations," and "A Breeze from Alabama." The World's Fair year brought "Cascades Rag" and "The Chrysanthemum: An Afro-American Intermezzo." Collaborating with Arthur Marshall, Joplin issued "Swipesey Cake Walk" in 1901, "Felicity Rag" (1911), and "Kismet Rag" (1913). "Heliotrope Bouquet Rag" was concocted with Louis Chauvin, his youthful protégé. Stark published "Augustan Club Waltzes" (1901), "March Majestic" (1902), "Rosebud March" (1905), and "Antoinette March" (1906). Late Stark rags are "Ragtime Dance" (1906), "Nonpareil Rag" (1907), "Fig Leaf Rag" (1908), "Magnetic Rag" (1914), and "Reflection Rag" (1917). Scott Joplin also wrote *The School of Ragtime* that Stark published in 1908. After the World's Fair, Joplin wrote many pieces for eastern publishers, notably "Sycamore: A Concert Rag" (1904), "Eugenia Rag" (1905), "Gladiolus Rag," "Rose Leaf Rag," "Searchlight Rag," "Pineapple Rag," and "Sugar Cane Rag" (all 1907), "Paragon Rag," "Wall Street Rag," "Country Club Rag," and "Euphonic Sounds Rag" (1909), and "Stoptime Rag" (1910).

Joplin's success as a ragtime composer enabled him to buy a thirteen-room house at 2117 Lucas Avenue in 1903. By 1906, his domestic life floundered and he became separated from his wife Belle. He sold his house to Arthur Marshall and went to Chicago. In 1907 he went to New York where he married Lottie Stokes in 1909.

Besides composing many piano pieces, Joplin also created two operas. The first, *The Guest of Honor*, was given a rehearsal production in St. Louis in 1903. It was copyrighted the same year and was to have been published in piano score by Stark. Unfortunately, the manuscript seems to have become lost in the mail. A second opera, *Treemonisha*, was published at his own expense in New York in 1911. It was eventually produced at a rehearsal performance in Harlem in 1915, but seems not to have been very successful. The failure of both operas was a tragic blow for Joplin, who really had high aspirations. He died in New York on 1 April 1917.

Meanwhile, another ragtime genius put in his appearance. James Scott was born in Neosho, Missouri in 1886 and spent his early years in Carthage. At age nineteen he came to St. Louis and started to compose. John Stark published his "Frog Legs Rag" in 1906. "Kansas City Rag" followed in 1907, "Grace and Beauty Rag," "Hilarity Rag," and "Ophelia Rag" in 1910, "Quality Rag" in 1914, "Evergreen Rag" in 1915, "Honeymoon Rag" and "Prosperity Rag" in 1916, "Efficiency Rag" and "Paramount Rag" in 1917, "Rag Sentimentale" in 1918, "New Era Rag," "Troubador Rag," and "Princess Rag" in 1919, "Pegasus Rag" and "Modesty Rag" in 1920, "Don't Jazz Me Rag" and "Victory Rag" in 1921, and "Broadway Rag" in 1922.

Another gifted black composer whose pieces Stark published was Arthur Marshall. Marshall was born in Saline County, Missouri, on 20 November 1881. He went to school with Scott Hayden in Sedalia. While Scott Joplin stayed at the Marshall home, he helped Arthur with his early compositions. When Joplin left St. Louis, Marshall bought his home. Marshall followed Joplin to Chicago and played in different saloons. Marshall was not a prolific composer. Stark published "Kinklets Two Step" in 1906, "Ham and -- : Rag," "Pippin Rag," and "Peach Ragtime Two Step" in 1908.

Artie Matthews was another gifted black genius. He was born in Minonk, Illinois in 1888. He was a very good reader and had great facility in notating music. He was very helpful in writing down the music of his friends. When Stark demanded something to offset "St. Louis Blues," Matthews came up with "Weary Blues" which really sold very well. Stark published all of Matthews' ragtime pieces, which were uniformly designated "Pastime Rag," numbers 1 to 5. He also composed seven ragtime songs of which four were published by the Princess Music Company, two by Seals & Feathers, and one by Thiebes-Stierlin Music Company.

While Stark had his New York office, he became acquainted with the work of Joseph Francis Lamb, a Caucasian who composed ragtime with the facility of a black. Stark published in St. Louis "Sensation Rag" in 1908, "Excelsior Rag" and "Ethiopian Rag" in 1909, "Champagne Rag" in 1910, "American Beauty Rag" in 1913, "Cleopatra Rag," "Contentment Rag," "Ragtime Nightingale," and "Reindeer Ragtime Two Step" in 1915, "Patricia Rag" and "Top-Liner Rag" in 1916, and finally "Bohemian Rag" in 1919. Lamb also composed about thirty rags that were never published.

In addition to the rags mentioned, John Stark & Son published some fifty ragtime pieces by twenty-five other composers. To give an idea of the extent of the Stark catalog, he also published fifty songs, fifty teaching pieces, thirty two-steps, and twenty waltzes. Needless to say, everything Stark published was permeated with the new syncopated rhythm or it would not have been published. John Stark died in St. Louis on 20 November 1927, in his eighty-sixth year.

Among the other St. Louis publishers who printed ragtime pieces we could mention Robert de Yong & Company of 916 Olive Street, who published Tom Turpin's "Harlem Rag" in 1897. They also published his "Bowery Buck Rag" in 1899 and "Ragtime Nightmare" in 1900. His "St. Louis Rag" and "Buffalo Rag" were published in Chicago in 1903 and 1904. "Siwash Indian Rag Intermezzo," "Pan-Am Rag," and "When Sambo Goes to France" remain in manuscript.

In 1903, Val Reis Music Company published "Weeping Willow: Ragtime Two Step" of Scott Joplin (Fig. 19), as well as "Something Doing Rag" contrived by Joplin and Scott Hayden. The T. Bahnsen Piano Manufacturing Company in 1905 produced "Binks Waltz" and "Bethena Concert Waltz," as well as the song "Sarah Dear," all three by Scott Joplin. "Lily Rag," another Joplin effusion, was printed by the Syndicate Music Company in 1914. Joplin's "Cleopha Two Step" was published by S. Simon in 1902, and his song "I'm Thinking of My Pickaninny Days" was put forth by Thiebes-Stierlin Music Company in 1914.

Charles Humfeld's "That Left Hand Rag" was published by Humfeld & Stark in 1912, Charles Drumheller's "Banjo Twang" by Drumheller & Reis in 1893, Joe Jordan's "Double Fudge Rag" by J. F. Hunleth in 1902, Lucian Gibson's "Jinx Rag" by Gibson & Stark in 1911-15, Robert Bircher's "Candy Rag" by Bircher in 1909, Scott Joplin's song "Snoring Sampson" by Universal Music Company (date not known), Thomas Shea's "Corinthian Rag" and "Oliver Road Rag" by Thiebes-Stierlin in 1914, and Gus Haenschen's "St. Louis Society Dance" by W. G. H. Haenschen in 1911. "Robardina Rag" by E. Warren Furry, arranged by Arthur B. Money, was copyrighted by Furry in 1902 and published by Balmer & Weber. Hubert Bauersachs, the brilliant violinist, tried his hand at ragtime and composed and published "Melrose Rag" and "Deuces Wild Rag" in 1922.

REFERENCE

R. Blesh and H. Janis, *They All Played Ragtime* (New York: Oak, 1950; rev. 1966).

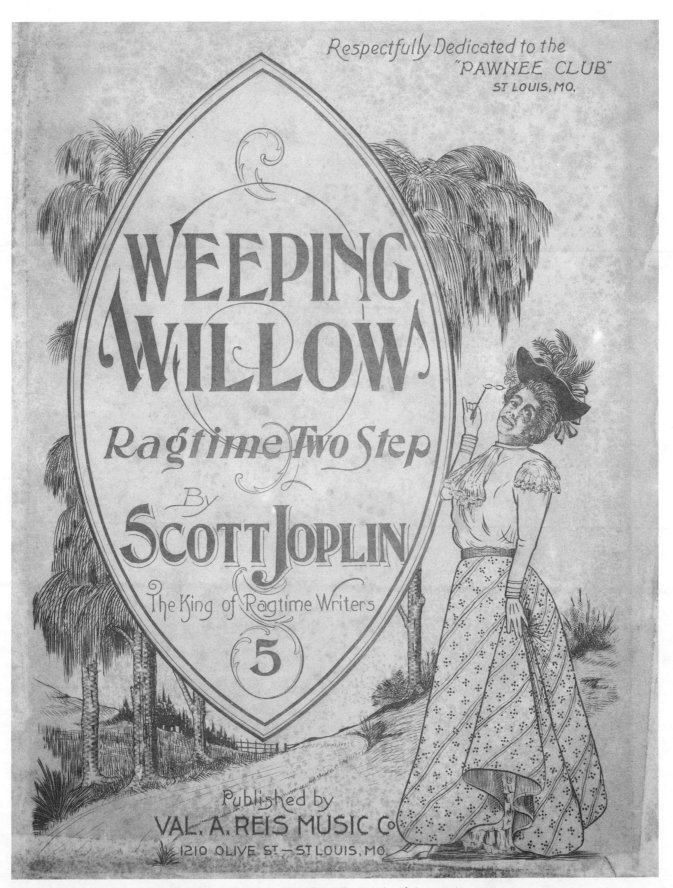

Fig. 19. Scott Joplin, Weeping Willow: Ragtime Two Step (St. Louis: Val A. Reis, 1903), title-page

18

THE TURN OF THE CENTURY

Frederick Charles Stierlin was a native son, born 10 October 1863,[1] of Henry J. and Amanda Weleker Stierlin. He attended Marquam College in Bloomington, Illinois for seven years, and graduated from Foster Academy in St. Louis in 1882. He began his business career as assistant bookkeeper at the Christian Pepper Tobacco Company. From 1888 to 1893 he was chief bookkeeper of Dozier Baker Company. He entered the music business as vice-president and treasurer of Thiebes-Stierlin Music Company in 1893. When the firm changed to Stierlin Piano Company in 1907 he functioned as president. He was also president of the Koerber-Brenner Music Company, jobbers in musical instruments.

Thiebes-Stierlin Music Company had a store at 1111 Olive Street in 1895 but moved to 1118 Olive Street the next year. By 1905 the store had been moved to 1006 Olive Street.

The greater part of the Thiebes-Stierlin catalog consisted of reprints of frequently-used piano pieces. The composers commonly duplicated were:

Joseph Ascher
C. Bachman
Franz Behr
Franz Bendel
Bluenberg
Luigi Boccherini
Carl Bohm
Cecile Chaminade
Frederic Chopin
Joseph Concone
W. Cooper
Theodore Döhler
Arnold Dolmetsch
August Durand
Richard Eilenberg
Giese
Jean Louis Gobbaerts (pseudonyms: Levy, Ludovic, Streabbog)
Benjamin Godard
Louis Moreau Gottschalk
Edvard Grieg
Salomon Jadassohn
Gustave Lange
Ignace Leybach
Pietro Mascagni
Felix Mendelssohn
G. A. Osborne
Josef Adalbert Pacher

---

1. *Book of St. Louisans* (St. Louis, 1912), 574.

Ignace Paderewski
Henri Ravina
Anton Rubinstein
Schirmer
Heinrich Schmidt
Wilhelm Schuster
Edward Schytte
François Thomé
Paul Wachs
Wachtman
Winter
Hermann Adolf Wollenhaupt

Many studies and etudes were also reprinted, most of them by Jacob Adelung, Joseph Ascher, Henry Bertini, Johann Burgmüller, Carl Czerny, Anton Diabelli, Jean Duvernoy, Louis Köhler, Albert Loeschhorn, and Heinrich Schmidt. A novel enrichment of the catalog was a group of vocal duets by Franz Abt, John Bernett, Vincenzo Bellini, Fabio Campana, Giacomo Donizetti, Fricker, Stephen Glover, Ferdinand Gumbert, and Anton Hackel.

The most important part of the catalog consisted of those works that were originally written for Thiebes-Stierlin and copyrighted by them and provided with a plate number. Of the compositions hereafter listed, copies are available in Gaylord Music Library. This list will be fairly extensive, for it is desired to include the title, the copyright date, and the plate number:

Sam Aronson, "I Love My Harp: Meditation" (1913), plate number 163-4; title-page (hereafter, t.p.) + 4 plates
Henry Bollman, "Convent Bells: Reverie" (1895), no pl. no.; t.p. + 7 pl. (imperfect)
Henry Bollman, "Convent Bells," new revised edition (1905), pl. no. 17-7; collective t.p. + 7 pl.
Gustav Ehrlich, "Barcarole" (1903), pl. no. 1106-5; lacks t.p.; 5 pl.
Charles Galloway, "O, Mother Dear Jerusalem," song (1900), pl. no. 3848-5, t.p. + 5 pl.
M. A. Gunn, "For Thee Alone" (Murray-Vollmar Music Co.), no copyright date, no pl. no.; t.p. + 3 pl.
Charles Humfeld, "I Am for You" (Humfeld & Flynn) (1907), pl. no. 535(3); t.p. + 3 pl.
Carl Wilhelm Kern, "The Harp Player and His Son" (Thiebes Piano Co.) (1910), pl. no. 87-3; collective t.p. + 3 pl.
C. W. Kern, "Evening Shadows," op. 119 (1910), pl. no. 531-5; collective t.p. + 5 pl.
Ernest R. Kroeger, "An Indian Lament," op. 53, no. 7 (1902), pl. no. 1573-3; collective t.p. + 3 pl.
E. R. Kroeger, "I Will Praise Thee" (1904), pl. no. 6055-10; collective t.p. + 10 pl., octavo
Arthur Lieber, "On the Stair" (1918), pl. no. 16-3; t.p. + 3 pl.
A. Lieber, "The Little Brown Feet of Oyaimo" (1907), pl. no. 625-3; no t.p., 3 pl.
Donald Lowmiller, "Old Time Favorites: Medley" (1912), pl. no. 596-5; t.p. + 5 pl.
Edwin Vaile McIntyre, "Among the Flowers" (1901), pl. no. 955-2; collective t.p. + 2 pl.
Cora D. Rohland, "The Day of Resurrection: Easter Carol" (1895), no pl. no.; t.p. + 2 pl., octavo
Henry Stanley Walser, "Grand Parade March" (1907), pl. no. 507-4; t.p. + 4 pl.

Louis Retter was another native son, born 29 April 1869.[2] His parents were Charles and Teresa Retter. He attended Christian Brothers College and eventually went to the Royal Conservatory of Music in Munich. On his return from Germany he taught violin, piano, and harmony privately. For eight years he was violinist in the St. Louis Symphony Orchestra.

---

2. Krohn, *Missouri Music* (New York, 1972), 124 and 365.

Retter was an outstanding composer and published his music as the Louis Retter Music Company. His catalog was diversified by the use of several *noms de plume*, notably Jean Becker, Emile de Bar, Theodore Keil, Arthur Listeman, Luch Nord, and Carl Sontag.

Outstanding publications were the *Louis Retter Melodious Piano Course* in four volumes, the *Louis Retter Melodious Violin Course* in several volumes, and the *Arthur Listeman Graded Piano Technics* in two volumes. His two "Airs concertantes" for violin and piano were published by Shattinger. He composed twelve vocal numbers for the Pageant and Masque of the Children of America Loyalty League that had three performances at the Odeon in 1919.

The catalog of Louis Retter is unique in that it consists mostly of original compositions but disguised by the use of several pseudonyms. Since a catalog is not available, the few reprints of standard pieces will only be noticed on collective title-pages.

The music in the Gaylord Music Library is listed under Retter and the various *noms de plume*. The original Retter compositions are:

"Francesca" (1902), pl. no. 64-3; t.p. + 3 pl.
"The Countess: Valse Lente" (1909), pl. no. 1077-6; t.p. + 6 pl.
"Two Hearts" (1912), pl. no. 1907-4; t.p. + 5 pl.
"Venetian Barcarolle," a song (1917), pl. no. 1100-4; t.p. + 4 pl.
"Deep River," transcription (1927), pl. no. 316-4; collective t.p. + 4 pl.

The pieces under pseudonyms:

Jean Becker, "Forsaken: Reverie" (1898), pl. no. 98-6; collective t.p. + 6 pl.
Emile de Bar, "Japanese Nightingale: A Spring Idylle" (1904), pl. no. 1001-4; t.p. + 4 pl.
Theodore Keil, "Evening Prayer: Reverie" (1897), pl. no. 105-3; collective t.p. + 3 pl.
Theodore Keil, "Scales and Chords" (1899), pl. no. 7-6; t.p. + 6 pl.
Carl Sontag, "Flower Waltz," transcription (1906), pl. no. 1029-3; t.p. + 3 pl.

Among the miscellaneous compositions are:

Carl Fedlerman, "Sunbeams on the Meadow: A Spring Reverie" (1907), pl. no. 1052-6; collective t.p. + 6 pl.
Franz Lehar, "Merry Widow Waltzes," transcriptions (1908), pl. no. 1080; t.p. + 6 pl.

Another native son, Valentine Anthony Reis, was born 20 September 1874, of Bartholomew Reis and Bernardine Steinweh Reis. He attended the public schools and a business college. At the age of eighteen he owned a news and book depot that he operated until 1912. He began to sell musical instruments in 1898, and incorporated his business in 1907 as the Val Reis Music Company. He had a store at 1010 Olive Street in 1900 but moved to 1210 Olive Street in 1902. When he incorporated he opened a larger store at 1005 Olive Street, where he remained until 1915. He published easy teaching pieces, but none seems to have survived. He eventually sold out to Shattinger.

Hubert Theodore Bauersachs was a native son who was born here 5 May 1882. He studied with J. P. Nemours, Guido Parisi, Paul Mori, and Louis Conrath. He became an outstanding violin virtuoso and was a prolific composer of music for violin and piano. He was partial to the form of the waltz. He published "Valse de concert"; "Valse brillante," no. 1; "My Own Valse," no. 13; and "Valses," opus 33, no. 7; opus 34, no. 8; opus 37, no. 11; and opus 40, no. 14. He also wrote a "Gavotte," no. 9; "Gavotte" in C, no. 17; "Tarantella"; and several "Mazurkas," nos. 3, 4, 15; a "Mazurka brillante," and "Mazurka d'artistes." Among his romantic pieces are: "A Dream," "Twilight," "Cradle Song," "Gondoliera," "Drifting," "Mother's Love," "Zephyr," "Fantasioso Caprice," "Momento musicale," "Berceuse," "Un Sogno," "Adagio cantabile," "Suena de Espana," "Espagnola Serenata," "Poesia de amor," "Suesses Erwarten," "Trueue Herzen," and a very difficult "Desiderio del Demonio." He also composed a very attractive "Liebeslied" for two violins and piano.

Walter Luhn was the publisher of *The Musical News* with editorial offices at Henneman Hall, 3723 Olive Street. It did not last very long. My father, Ernst Ludwig Krohn, was his assistant editor and I had charge of the subscription lists. *The Musical News* consisted of full-length articles and several pieces of music in each issue. A complete bound copy is in the Gaylord Music Library. Several pieces have survived individually. Two 1896 copyrights are "La Parade March" and "Funny Fellow March." "Louise Waltz" was an 1899 copyright. All three were composed by Luhn.

Luhn eventually gave up music and became a medical doctor. His specialty seems to have been marrying wealthy widows. So soon as his wife discovered his true nature she divorced him, but he always found someone else.

19

MUSIC AND THE WORLD'S FAIR

The night was balmy, the deepening darkness was made luminous by the myriads of lights that outlined the nearby buildings, the atmosphere was drenched with sound, for the Banda Rosa was playing a Wagner program. Snugly ensconced in one of the commodious band stands that occurred here and there, the resonant brasses reproduced to perfection the vast sonorities of the Wagnerian music.[1] The Banda Rosa, conducted by Eugenio Sorrentino, consisted of fifty musicians, every man an artist.[2] This was the golden age of the brass band during which individual bands surpassed many a symphony orchestra in perfection of finish and tremendous expressiveness.

In addition to the Italian Banda Rosa, there were the French Garde Republicaine Band, the British Grenadier Guards Band, the German Philharmonisches Blas Orchester of Berlin, the Canadian Victoria Band, the President's Band of Mexico, the Philippine Constabulary Band, the Philippine Scouts Band, the U.S. Marine Band, the Boston Band, the Haskell Indian School Band, and the Kilties' Band.[3] Then there were the individual bands led by such conductors as John Philip Sousa,[4] Frederick Neil Innes,[5] Francesco Fanciulli,[6] John C. Weber,[7] Frederick Phinney, William Weil,[8] Luciano Contero,[9] and Ellery, not to mention the numerous state and regimental bands.[10] There were six handsome band pavilions scattered here and there, and they were usually in continuous use.

The Bureau of Music was efficiently conducted by George D. Markham of St. Louis, and he was ably assisted by George D. Stewart as Manager and Ernest R. Kroeger as Master of

---

1. Partly autobiographical. I was there. See also D. R. Francis, *The Universal Exposition of 1904*, 2 vols. (St. Louis, 1913), 1:79, 255.

2. See H. W. Schwartz, *Bands of America* (New York, 1957), 212, 239.

3. Schwartz, 203-06; also Francis, 1:193-95.

4. See DAB 17:407-08; also J. P. Sousa, *Marching Along* (New York, 1928).

5. See G. Bridges, *Pioneers in Brass* (Detroit, 1965), 94-96; also C. Saerchinger, *International Who's Who in Music* (New York, 1918), 300.

6. Saerchinger, 183; G. E. Schiavo, *Italian-American History*, 2 vols. (New York, 1947), 1:319-20; *Baker's Biographical Dictionary of Musicians*, 4th ed. (1940), 324.

7. See M. H. Osburn, *Ohio Composers and Musical Authors* (Columbus, 1942), 197.

8. Schwartz, 163.

9. Schiavo, 1:298-99.

10. Francis, 1:194-95.

Programs.[11] The bureau engaged a symphony orchestra composed of sixty-two musicians who gave twenty-five symphony concerts in Festival Hall[12] and daily popular programs in the Tyrolean Alps[13] for the duration of the exposition.[14] Among the directors were Max Bendix,[15] Walter Damrosch,[16] Alfred Ernst,[17] Nahan Franco,[18] Joseph Helmesberger,[19] Richard Heuberger,[20] Karl Komzak,[21] Emil Mollenhauer,[22] Frank Van der Stucken,[23] and Max Zach.[24]

Festival Hall housed a tremendous five-manual organ that had been especially constructed for the World's Fair.[25] Charles Galloway was official organist and he directed the programming of organ recitals by visiting organists from the rest of the world. Outstanding was the engagement of Alexandre Guilmant, the famous French organist,[26] who gave some forty recitals that were very well attended.[27]

On 29 June 1904, the Treble Cleff Club of Leavenworth, Kansas, and the Kansas City Symphony Orchestra gave *King Olaf* by Carl Busch, the composer conducting. *The Creation* by Joseph Haydn was performed by the Dubuque Choral Society under the baton of W. I. Pontius on July 11. Handel's *Messiah* was presented July 9 by the St. Louis Choral Symphony Society assisted by the Morning Choral and the Apollo Club with Alfred Ernst conducting. The com-

---

11. Francis, 1:192.

12. Photographs in Francis, 2:201, 289, 295.

13. Francis, 1:594; photograph, 2:77.

14. Francis, 1:193-94.

15. See Saerchinger, 53; *Baker's*, 4th ed. (1940), 90.

16. See *Baker's*, 5th ed. (1958), 345; also W. Damrosch, *My Musical Life* (New York, 1924).

17. See Krohn, *Century of Missouri Music* (St. Louis, 1924), 108.

18. See Saerchinger, 201.

19. See *Grove's Dictionary of Music and Musicians*, 5th ed. (1954), 4:230; *Riemanns Musik Lexikon*, 11th ed. (Berlin, 1929): 1:733; *Musik in Geschichte und Gegenwart* (henceforth, MGG), 6:115.

20. MGG 6:334; Riemann, 1:752; *Grove's*, 4:265; *Baker's*, 707.

21. See *Grove's*, 4:818.

22. See DAB, 13:80; also *Baker's*, 1101.

23. *Baker's*, 1686; also DAB, 19:181-82.

24. DAB, 20:639-40; Krohn, *Century*, 134; *Baker's*, 1834.

25. See Francis, 1:195.

26. See *Baker's*, 626-27.

27. See Francis, 1:195. [A photograph of Guilmant at the organ is in Orpha Ochse, *The History of the Organ in the United States* (Bloomington, 1975), 359. —Ed.]

bined Evanston and Ravenswood Choral Societies directed by Peter G. Lutkin produced *Caractacus* by Edward Elgar on July 13. The oratorio *Elijah* by Mendelssohn was sung July 16 by the Scranton Oratorio Society, with J. T. Watkins conducting.[28] In addition to the choral groups mentioned so far, the following organizations participated in the two prize contests that were staged: Denver Select Choir, Henry Housely, conductor; Denver Choral Society, Gwilym Thomas; Belleville Choral Society, Ludwig Carl; Colorado Oratorio Society, Claude Rossignol; Pittsburgh Cathedral Choir, Joseph Otten.[29]

This was the miracle of the Louisiana Purchase Exposition of 1904, that music groups from every cultural center of the civilized world thronged into St. Louis to participate in the exceedingly rich program of musical events. Magnificent music added its magic to the tremendous visual impression that overwhelmed one on every side.

The Louisiana Purchase Exposition was originally planned to open in May 1903. As the time approached, it was was found advisable to postpone the opening to 1904. Since the Liberal Arts Building was ready for use in 1903, the dedication program was held then.[30] The Nordamerikanischer Saengerbund was accustomed to holding a Saengerfest every second year. When the date was set in 1901 for the next Saengerfest, it was in the expectation that the World's Fair would be in session in 1903. The postponement of the exposition did not give the Saengerbund sufficient time to change its date, so that the Thirty-First Saengerfest was given in the Liberal Arts Building as originally planned.[31] The Twenty-Sixth Annual Meeting of the Music Teachers' National Association, Thomas A. Becket, president, was duly held in 1904.[32] The Missouri Music Teachers' Association, T. Carl Whitmer, president, also convened in St. Louis during June of 1904.[33]

Of the music specifically composed for the World's Fair, the most important was *Hymn of the West*, a choral composition by John Knowles Paine[34] to the poem of Edmund Clarence Stedman.[35] This poem was sung during the program on opening day, 30 April 1904, by a chorus of four hundred voices conducted by Alfred Ernst, conductor of the St. Louis Choral Symphony Orchestra. The surviving music is an arrangement for vocal solo with piano accompaniment that was published and copyrighted by Thiebes-Stierlin Music Company in 1904.[36] The very elaborate title-page was designed by Vernon Howe Bailey but was copyrighted by Robert Allen Reid. Under an arch and in the background stands Festival Hall and its adjoining peristyles. Under the arch is grouped a large concourse of Indians, Spaniards, Frenchmen, and fron-

28. See Francis, 1:196.

29. Francis, 1:94-95.

30. Francis, 1:134-54.

31. See *Souvenir Program Book of the 33. Saengerfest* (Milwaukee, 1911), 16.

32. See *Papers and Proceedings of the MTNA*, 28th Annual Meeting, p. 200.

33. See *Official Reports MTNA*, 21st Annual Meeting (1916), 5.

34. See DAB, 14:151-53; also *Baker's*, 5th ed. (1958), 1199. [See also John C. Schmidt, *The Life and World of John Knowles Paine* (Ann Arbor: UMI Research Press, 1980), 188-89, 447-48. —Ed.]

35. See DAB, 17:552-53; also J. D. Hart, *Oxford Companion to American Literature* (New York, 1965), 799-800.

36. Copy in MHS; title-page, 3 plates of descriptive matter, and 5 plates of music numbered 1089-5.

tiersmen, and immediately in front of them stands a monk who seems to be directing them in song.

The other work composed specifically for the occasion is "Louisiana March,"[37] composed by Frank Van der Stucken[38] and performed on the same opening day program by Sousa's Band. The piano transcription of this march was published by Thiebes-Stierlin Music Company in 1904, although it was copyrighted by R. A. Reid. In the course of the march, Van der Stucken used snatches of the "Marsellaise," "Dixie," "Hail Columbia," and "Old Hundred." The title-page presents a full page view of the St. Louis Plaza[39] with the Louisiana Monument, and was designed by Vernon H. Bailey. A stunning drawing by Bailey of Festival Hall and the Cascades adorns the title-page of "Along the Plaza Waltzes,"[40] composed by Henry Kimball Hadley[41] and dedicated to the Board of Lady Managers (Fig. 20). It was again published by Thiebes-Stierlin Music Company, and copyrighted by R. A. Reid, in 1904. Each of the preceding publications was designated "Official Music Publication, Louisiana Purchase Exposition, St. Louis, 1904."

Louis Conrath[42] composed a difficult piano piece that he named "La Cascade (Impromptu)."[43] It was published and copyrighted by Kunkel Brothers in 1904 and bore on the title-page an attractive picture of Festival Hall and the Cascades. Scott Joplin[44] contributed "Cascades Rag," which was published by John Stark & Son in 1904.[45] "Festival Hall Waltzes" was composed by Glenn W. Ashleigh but was published and copyrighted in Chicago by Victor Kremer Company.[46] The striking picture of Festival Hall on the title-page was printed in blue and black. "The Hostess Waltzes" were written by William F. Hoffman who dedicated them to the "Hostesses of the Louisiana Purchase Exposition."[47] It has an attractive title-page and was published and copyrighted by G. W. Mogelberg Company of St. Louis in 1904. Bert Morgan composed "Louisiana Purchase Exposition March and Two Step" which he dedicated to the "New St. Louis."[48] It was published and copyrighted by M. P. Koch & Company of St. Louis in 1902.

37. Copy in MHS; title-page of descriptive matter + 14 plates of music numbered 1382-14.

38. See DAB, 19:181-82; also *Baker's*, 1686.

39. See Francis, 2:197.

40. Copy in GML; title-page, 2 plates of text, and 10 plates of music numbered 721-10; for the Festival Hall, see Francis, 2:289.

41. See *Baker's*, 635-36.

42. See Krohn, *Century*, 106.

43. Copy in GML; title-page + 7 plates of music numbered 1922-7.

44. See R. Blesh and H. Janis, *They All Played Ragtime* (New York, 1950; rev. 1966), 35-45 [or 4th ed., 1977, pp. 35-50 —Ed.]; *The ASCAP Biographical Dictionary* (New York, 1966), 374; *Baker's 1965 Supplement*, 63.

45. Copy in collection of Tibor Tichenor; title-page + 4 plates of music.

46. Copy in GML; title-page + 6 plates of music.

47. Copy in GML; title-page + 6 plates of music.

48. Copy in MHS; title-page + 4 plates of music.

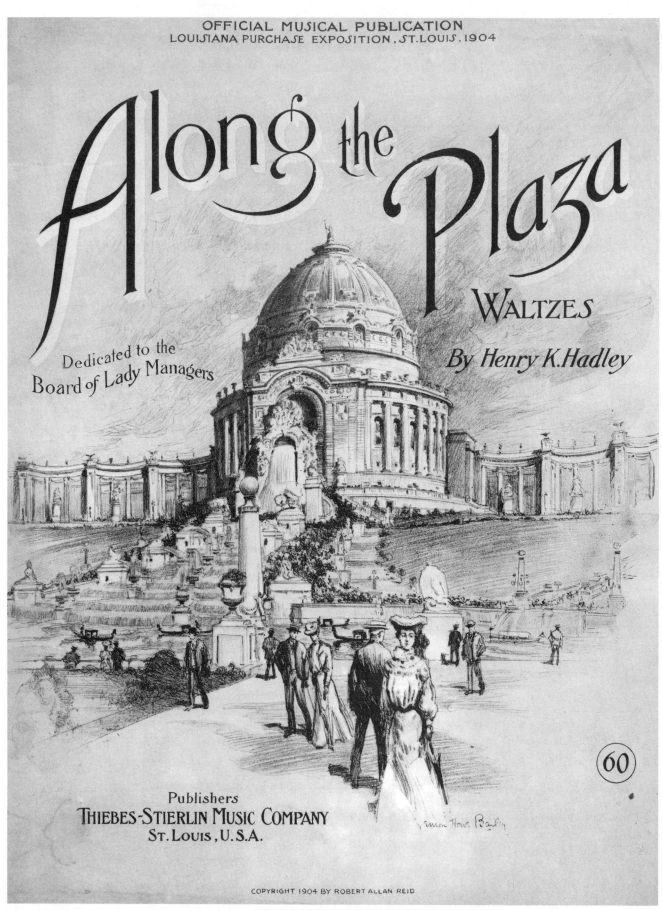

Fig. 20. Henry K. Hadley, Along the Plaza Waltzes (St. Louis: Thiebes-Stierlin, 1904), title-page

The title-page is embellished with the portraits of Mayor Rolla Wells[49] and Exposition President David R. Francis.[50]

The most popular piece connected with the World's Fair was the sensational song hit "Meet Me in St. Louis, Louis, Meet Me at the Fair."[51] The music was composed by Kerry Mills[52] to appropriate words by Andrew B. Sterling,[53] and the composition was published and copyrighted in 1904 by its composer, F. A. Mills of New York City. This practically became the theme song of the Fair, and was sung everywhere.

Another song, but not so popular, was published and copyrighted in 1904 by G. Venturini of the Italian section, Liberal Arts Building. The title "Yes, My Love,"[54] the music by Vincenzo Valenet to words by Eleanor Record, bore no relation to the World's Fair, although the title-page carries a small picture of the Liberal Arts Building.

---

49. Mayor of St. Louis during the World's Fair years.

50. See DAB, 6:577-78; president of the Louisiana Purchase Exposition Company and author of *The Universal Exposition of 1904* (see note 1, above).

51. Copy in GML; title-page, one plate of text, and 3 plates of music.

52. Frederick Allen (Kerry) Mills; see *ASCAP Biographical Dictionary*, 513.

53. *ASCAP Biographical Dictionary*, 706.

54. Copy in GML; title-page + 4 plates of music.

20

AN EDUCATIONAL ADVENTURE

An educational adventure that had far-reaching possibilities was inaugurated in St. Louis in 1912. Two Texas businessmen conceived the idea of creating a course of study for piano with integrated theoretical study that would standardize the teaching of both subjects. These men were John Philip Blake and Roman Simeon Waldron.

Waldron was born in Florida, 11 May 1871. He represented a British syndicate buying land in the U.S. He eventually settled in Galveston and was prospering in the real estate business when the Galveston flood of 1900 wiped him out. He went to Dallas and was recouping his finances when he met Blake. They became good friends and entered into a business partnership. Waldron was to remain in the real estate business while Blake went into music publishing.

Blake was born in Chatham, New Brunswick, Canada, 13 August 1867. His family moved to Chicago and he attended the public schools through high school. He became connected with the West Publishing House in Chicago and eventually became a reporter on the *Chicago Times*. In his twenties he went to San Francisco and entered the textbook business. He next went to Denver and remained in the publishing business. In the 1890s he sold out in Denver and went to Fort Worth and invested in real estate. The panic of 1893 wiped him out financially. He eventually got into the piano business and prospered. He established himself in Dallas in the publishing business as the Columbian Conservatory of Music. This may have been a correspondence course. Some of the music has survived, notably "Moments musical" by Schubert, "The Knight of Old" by Friedrich Robert Volkman, "To the Distant Beloved" by Hugo Reinhold, and "The Song of the Lark" by Tchaikovsky. All of these pieces had supplementary sheets of Biography, Interpretation, Theoretical Analysis, Structure, and Examination Questions. These pieces are all copyrighted by the Columbian Conservatory of Music, 1910-12.

The first piece bearing the imprint of the Art Publication Society seems to be "Hearts Amulet" by H. F. Engleman, but copyrighted by the Columbian Conservatory in 1911. All of these surviving pieces have interesting title-pages.

Blake eventually went to St. Louis and continued in business as the Crown Publishing Company. Three pieces have survived. They are "Frisky Galop" and "Pansy Polka" by Streabbog, and "Light Hearted: A Polka" by François [Franz] Behr. From the collective title-pages we can pick up some more titles: "Ivy Branch," "Playfulness," "Woodbine Schottisch," "Little Fairy Waltz," "Little Fairy March," "Minnie Waltz," and "Honeysuckle Waltz," all by Streabbog. He also published a "Menuet" by Mozart, and "L'Invitation à la valse" by Weber with a title-page that lists Dallas as well as St. Louis.

It may have been at this time that Waldron and Blake conceived the idea of reconstructing music teaching. They discussed the matter with their business friends who contributed to a fund to explore the possibilities of their novel conception. They engaged W. S. B. Mathews, the music critic, to do some research. He recommended that they engage an editor-in-chief and suggested Leopold Godowsky for the position. Godowsky was willing to accept the job provided they gave him as co-editors Josef Hofmann, Emil von Sauer, Edgar Stillman Kelley, Emerson Whithorne, and Cecil Forsythe. They got together and proceeded to write a Course of Study. Whithorne wrote on "Ear Training," Kelley on "Harmony," Forsythe on "History," and Godowsky and Hofmann on "Principles of Piano Playing."

At this time, the project became known as the Progressive Series Plan of Music Education, and the publisher was known as the Art Publication Society. Due to its central location and its excellent printing facilities, St. Louis was selected as publication headquarters. The offices were first located at 207 North Third Street, then at 1000 North Grand Avenue. In 1916, the offices were removed to 916 Olive Street, and in 1919 a change was made to 4517-19 Olive Street. Finally, in 1929, publication headquarters were removed to 7801 Bonhomme Avenue and the St. Louis Institute of Music was established at the same address in Clayton.[1]

Leopold Godowsky was editor-in-chief from 1912 until his death in 1938. Obviously, Godowsky could not be chained to a desk in St. Louis permanently. Actually, he visited headquarters only about once a year. In order to carry on the editorial work in St. Louis it was necessary to have an executive editor to control the local situation. Frederic Lillebridge functioned as executive editor from 1912 to 1914. He was succeeded by the well-known composer Emerson Whithorne from 1915 to 1919. In 1919, Arthur Edward Johnstone assumed the office. Johnstone was an editorial expert, having been on the staff of the American Book Company. He was also a gifted composer and theoretician. His revision of the course of study was fundamental and exceedingly thorough. He retired in 1939 and was succeeded by Louis Victor Saar, a choral composer who had won numerous prizes for his secular cantatas. Saar died of an ear infection within a few years. He was succeeded by Lillie Mayes Dodd, who served until 1951. Charles P. Mitchell functioned from 1951 until his death 15 April 1961. Robert Adams succeeded Mitchell in 1962 and was active through 1967. The editor following him was Graham Hollobom, who retired in July 1971.

The Course of Study of the Progressive Series has been revised and rewritten a half-dozen times. The individual pieces are laid out according to a definite plan. After the text of the piano piece is found a page of formal analysis and a story of the romantic context of the piece. This is followed by pages of theoretical exposition, with finally a page of definitions and another of examination questions. These were to be answered and sent to the editorial office for grading. Lillie Mayes Dodd functioned as examiner for many years.

The title-page was embellished with the portrait of the composer. This made for a dreadful uniformity in the appearance of all of the piano pieces. Such deadly standardization was the inescapable result of the effort to create a homogeneous course of study. Practically all of the music plates were engraved by Edward J. Steiner and the music was printed in the plant of the Art Publication Society.

Since an executive editor could not handle all of the details of publication, it was necessary to engage numerous contributing editors. Closely connected with the work in its early stages were Alexander Henneman, Lillie Mayes Dodd as examiner, and Lillian Vandevere as elementary editor. Inasmuch as the publications included not only the Progressive Series of Piano Studies but innumerable supplementary piano pieces, it was necessary to engage editors for these pieces. Outstanding among these were Ernest Richard Kroeger, Frank M. Webster, Gottfried Galston, and Ernst C. Krohn.

---

1. Information pertaining to the inner history of the Art Publication Society was supplied by John P. Blake.

Fig. 21. *Mel Bay's Modern Guitar Method: Grade 1* (Pacific, Mo.: Mel Bay, 1972), cover

21

MEL BAY: A POTENT TRADEMARK

The most comprehensive system of studies for the plucked instruments was published by Mel Bay within the last twenty-five years. He has had a superb staff of collaborators, among them Mel Agen, Chet Atkins, Frank Bradbury, Vincent Bredice, Joseph Castle, Roger Erb, Roger Filiberto, David Gornston, Roger Holtman, Ronny Lee, Pat Masone, Sonny Osborne, Harry Volpe, Franz Zeidler, as well as his son Bill and his daughter Susan Bay Banks.[1]

Melbourne Earl Bay was born in Bunker, Missouri, 25 February 1913. In 1915 his parents moved to St. Louis but in 1925 they settled in De Soto. Nine years later they returned to St. Louis, where he has lived ever since. At fourteen he received a guitar for Christmas and taught himself to play. The Ozark fiddler Paul Hill helped him somewhat and he made such rapid progress that he was encouraged to take up the tenor banjo the next year. He began playing at parties and at dances in Jefferson and Washington counties, and at Crystal City, Festus, Old Mines, and Potosi. At eighteen he began taking banjo lessons from Bunny Longo at the Hugo Schools of Music in St. Louis. He was kept busy playing at hotels and ballrooms. He also played Hawaiian guitar at radio station KMOX. In the 1940s he began to teach at the Ludwig Schools of Music.

Bay's first book, the *Mel Bay Orchestral Chord System*, was published by the Louis Retter Music Company of St. Louis in 1947. The very next year he bought the copyright back and published under his own copyright claim. He married his pupil May Gebellein on 7 November 1937. Together they managed to produce the seven books of his *Modern Guitar Method*. Bay offered the manuscript to publishers in New York and Chicago, but to no avail. They would not have it, and he was forced to consider publishing at his own expense. The Louis Retter Music Company published the second book in 1949, but Bay bought it back the same year and proceeded on his own, publishing a book every year from 1948 to 1953. Up to 1972 he sold ten million copies of the *Modern Method*, which is an extraordinary performance (see Fig. 21).

The classical guitar is played with the fingers but without a plectrum, so that it would require a different approach. Mel Bay's *Classic Guitar Method* was originally produced in five books in 1955, but in the most recent edition it has been consolidated into three books, published in 1970-71. Joseph Castle edited three books of solos that were published as *Classic Guitar Solos* (volume 2) in 1964, *Classic Guitar Music* and *Easy Classic Guitar Solos* (volume 1) in 1971.

Many supplementary volumes appeared from time to time. Chet Atkins's two books *Style for Guitar* appeared in 1952 and 1964. Roger Filiberto compiled a book *Teenage Guitar Styles* in 1964, and he also contrived a book *Folk Guitar Styles* in 1967. The rich variety of *Flamenco Guitar Styles* was revealed by Mel Agen in 1971. Roger Erb and Roger Holtman collaborated in a book *Twelve-String Guitar Styles* in 1967. *Guitar Improvising* proved to be a fascinating work in two books, compiled by Vincent Bredice and published in 1969-70. Harry Volpe contributed a collection of difficult pieces entitled *The Guitar Virtuoso* in 1971. *Guitar Technic* was expertly explored by Roger Filiberto in 1972.

------

1. [William A. (Bill) Bay writes, January 1988, that a more up-to-date list would be Chet Atkins, Vincent Bredice, Craig Duncan, Robert Filiberto, Tommy Flint, Michael Lorimer, Joe Pass, and Tommy Tedesco. —Ed.]

Popular music received treatment in a series of specialized books. Ronny Lee published *Jazz Guitar Method* in two books in 1962-63. *Guitar in Gear* was offered by Pat Masone in 1967. Roger Filiberto contributed *Rockin' Rhythms for the Junior Guitarist* in 1964, and also compiled *Steel Guitar Method* in two books that came out in 1968-69. David Gornston was responsible for the two books *Swingin' Guitar* that were actually published by the Gate Music Company of New York in 1964-65, but were loaned to Mel Bay. Gornston also wrote *Guitar Rhythm Reader* that was published in 1967. An unusual *Blue Grass Banjo*, as interpreted by Sonny Osborne, was issued in 1964.

A book of *Guitar Ensembles* was arranged by Joseph Castle in 1960. Ronny Lee produced two books *Guitar Band* in 1959-60. *New Sounds for Electric Bass and Guitar* were provided by Roger Filiberto in 1970, and he also wrote two books for the *Electric Bass* in 1963 and 1965.

Mel Bay published several methods for other stringed instruments. Burton H. Isaac compiled a very extensive *String Method* that consists of two books each for violin, viola, cello, bass, and piano accompaniment, of which the first books were published in 1965 and the second in 1967. He also contrived a book *Folk Fiddle* that appeared in 1964. Frank Bradbury composed a *Five-String Banjo Method* in two volumes that came out in 1967. A *Mandolin Method* and a *Tenor Banjo Method* in two books each were published in 1968-69.

Books devoted to chords proved very useful. Mel Bay's first publication in 1947 was his ever-popular *Chord System*. He subsequently published *Guitar Chords* in 1959; *Banjo Chords*, *Tenor Banjo Chords*, *Ukelele Chords*, and *Baritone Uke Chords* in 1961; *Mandolin Chords* in 1963; and *Guitar Melody Chords* in 1966. Bill Bay compiled a magnificent *Deluxe Encyclopedia of Guitar Chords*, published in 1961.

An extensive series of *Fun Books* appeared from time to time. It all began with *Fun with the Guitar* in 1958. Then followed *Fun with the Ukelele* and *Fun with the Baritone Uke* in 1961, *Fun with the Five-String Banjo* and *Fun with the Tenor Banjo* in 1961, *Fun with the Mandolin* and *Fun with Folksongs* in 1963, *Fun with the Tenor Guitar* in 1964, and *Fun with the Banjo* in 1967. Bill Bay contributed six booklets in 1970-71: *Fun with the Violin, Clarinet, Flute, Trumpet, Trombone, Saxophone*. Bill Bay's sister Susan Bay Banks compiled *Fun with the Autoharp*, and Franz Zeidler *Fun with the Recorder*, both in 1971.[2]

The Mel Bay books are all published in the same format. The text varies from twenty to fifty-six pages, the general average being about forty-eight pages. The cover is a glossy white stiff cardboard, the size about nine by twelve inches.[3] The text is liberally interspersed with photographs of playing positions and diagrams of chord fingerings. The covers are printed in brilliant color, every book a different shade from its predecessor. The designs are artistically done and in very good taste. Nearly every cover has the reproduction in color of the instrument involved. The *Easy Way* covers are particularly attractive. No expense was spared to make the Mel Bay publications as attractive inwardly and outwardly as possible. Millions have been sold so far.

———

2. [More has been published, of course, since this was written. For the latest catalog, write Mel Bay Publications, 4 Industrial Dr., Pacific, MO 63069-0066. —Ed.]

3. [William Bay (see note 1) indicates that the publications now vary widely in size and number of pages, many of them spiral bound, and that a wide range of instruments is now covered. —Ed.]

Title Index

Title Index

Venetian Barcarolle (Retter), 92
Vesper Hymn to the Virgin, 56
Victory Rag (Scott), 87
Vienna Waltz (Winter), 72
Vienne Galop (Ketterer), 75
Violet Polka (Bishop), 56
Violet Waltz (Pollatscheck), 70
Vive la Dance, 44
Vive la Dance (Meyer), 19
Von Weber's Last Waltz (Bateman), 57

Wahr Will I Go if de War Breaks de Country Up? (Murphy), 62
Wait for the Waggon (Balmer), 56
Wall Street Rag (Joplin), 87
Wanderer (Schubert), 62, 73
Wanderer's Dream (Abt), 75
Warblings at Eve (Richards), 74
Water Witch: Valse Brillante (Werner), 52
Weary Blues (Matthews), 87
Webster's Funeral March (attrib. Beethoven), 42
Weeping Willow: Ragtime Two Step (Joplin), 88; Fig. 19
Weep Not Fond Heart (Kuecken), 73
Welcome Home Schottisch (Brunner), 70
We'll Meet Above (Liebe), 73-74
We Met by Chance (Kuecken), 75
Western Emigrant, 9
Western Journal, 9
What Are the Wild Waves Saying? (Glover), 64
What Are the Wild Waves Saying (Richards), 74
What in My Heart So Deep Unspoken (Gumbert), 64, 73
When Sambo Goes to France (Turpin), 88

When the Moonbeams Tender Light (Hodson), 44
When the Quiet Moon Is Beaming (Schorndorf), 75
When the Swallows Homeward Fly, 62
When the Swallows Homeward Fly (Oesten), 74
Where Roses Fair (Gustav), 75
White Rose (Coupa), 51
White Rose Schottisch, 64
Who Shall Be Fairest (Gumbert), 64
Wild Wood Birds, 57
Willie's Favorite Waltz (Brunner), 70
Winged Messengers (Fesca), 65
Winter Evening Waltz (Balmer), 45
Within a Mile of Edinboro Town, 62
Woodbine Schottisch (Streabbog/Gobbaerts), 100
Woodland Home Waltz (Bierman), 70
Worth of Time (Schobe), 26
Write a Letter from Home (Paoler), 51

Yankee Doodle, 40
Ye Merry Birds (Gumbert), 75
Yes, My Love (Valenet), 99
You Had Better Ask Me (Louis), 52
You'll See Dem on de Ohio (Guernsey), 31
Young Eph's Lamentation (Murphy), 62
You (Robyn), 74
Youth by the Brook (Proch), 73
You Think I Have a Merry Heart (Brunner), 76

Zauberflöte (Mozart), 72
Zehn Mädchen und kein Mann (Suppé), 68
Zephyr (Bauersachs), 92
Zephyr's Choice (Hine), 56

J. BUNKER CLARK, who prepared this book for publication, is professor of music history at the University of Kansas. He earned three degrees at the University of Michigan, and was a Fulbright scholar at Jesus College, Cambridge University, in 1962-63. His publications include Transposition in Seventeenth Century English Organ Accompaniments and the Transposing Organ *(this publisher, 1974),* Anthology of Early American Keyboard Music, 1787-1830 *(Recent Researches in American Music, vols. 1-2, 1977),* Nathaniel Giles: Anthems *(Early English Church Music, vol. 23, 1979), and* The Dawning of American Keyboard Music *(Greenwood Press, 1988). He has contributed to* Music & Letters, Musica Disciplina, Notes, Current Musicology, Fontes Artis Musicae, American Music, *and* The New Grove Dictionary of American Music. *With his wife Marilyn S. Clark, he was editor of this series in 1975-84, has been general editor for this publisher since 1982, and since 1985 has been the series editor of Detroit Studies in Music Bibliography.*